MW01714405

ꟹ SEC

Second-Hand Tuxedo

Trisha Field

Paula & Alan,
May God Bless you!!
Trisha Field
Phil 4:13

NORTH STAR PRESS OF ST. CLOUD, INC.
St. Cloud, Minnesota

Our thanks to Carrow's of Waite Park for use of the tuxedo shown on the cover.

ISBN-10: 0-87839-267-X
ISBN-13: 978-0-87839-4

First Edition: October 2007

Printed in the United States of America

Published by
North Star Press of St. Cloud, Inc.
P.O. Box 451
St. Cloud, Minnesota 56302

northstarpress.com
info@northstarpress.com

In memory of my mother,
Jeanette,
who taught me to dream big dreams
and never give up.

☙ 1 ❧

Pushing the empty bin into place, Matt, the manager of the Goodwill, glanced up. Another car was pulling into the drop off area.

I'm glad I covered the receiving area for this break, Matt thought. He watched as the car, a maroon Mercedes, neared. *Bet that's Mrs. M. for one of her drop-offs. Must be nice to drive that Mercedes. This is the eighth, no, maybe the tenth, drop-off from her in the six years I've been here.* Matt glanced back at one of his employees, looking for a candidate to process the clothing. *Evelyn's been moving slowly all day like she's a bit down. This'll cheer her up,* he thought with a smile.

The car came to a full stop. But instead of the beautiful woman in her late forties he was used to seeing make the drop-off, a man in his late fifties got out of the car. *The butler, I'll bet,* Matt thought sardonically, missing the obvious sadness in the man's eyes as the trunk popped open and the man walked to the back of the vehicle.

The trunk was full of clothing, much more than the woman usually dropped off, and then Matt saw that the back seat was full as well; the expensive car was, quite literally, stuffed. Matt pushed out an empty bin. Together, he and the man unloaded the clothing from the car and trunk, along with boxes of perfume and other personal items. When the last of it was in the bin, the man reached out and touched the pile. A tear ran down his cheek. By this time, Matt was busy getting the receipt and did not notice the deep emotions of the man's gesture.

As the man drove off, Matt pushed the bin inside. *I bet Evelyn'll like to see these right away*, he thought remembering how she always cheered up when the Mercedes stopped. Matt skipped the staging area and moved directly toward Evelyn.

Evelyn was deep in thought, sorting a rack of dresses and didn't hear Matt coming.

"You look depressed, Evelyn," Matt said gently.

She startled, then squared her shoulders. "I'm a Christian woman. I'm not supposed to be sad or depressed. After everything I've been through raising four kids since Jim passed away, why would the last one graduating from college make me so miserable?"

Matt didn't have an answer.

Evelyn half-heartedly moved the clothing around in the heat of the mid-summer day. The humidity was making her moodier as well as hot.

"Oh, how I wish people wouldn't put moth balls in the back of their closets," she muttered to Matt. "Freshly washed clothes means freshly washed and not packed for years in mothballs."

"No," Matt said, "but by tomorrow the smell will be blended with all the odors from all the other closets we get in here and you won't notice it."

"But I hate the smell of moth balls."

Matt ignored that. "Evelyn, I've got a surprise for you." Matt had kept the full bin just off to the side out of her sight as she was straightening up the rack of clothes.

"I'll be done here in a minute. Then I'll give you my full attention."

Matt waited, barely able to contain his glee in what he was about to show her.

Evelyn took a deep breath. The smell of fresh cedar from the Mercedes' woman's clothes was permeating the area. Evelyn's nose easily pointed her to Matt.

"Cedar? Someone with a cedar closet must have just dropped some clothes off," Evelyn stated as she finished her task.

"The Mercedes just came. They filled a bin all by themselves."

Matt's tantalization worked. Evelyn stopped working on the rack and followed him.

"Wow!" She said as she stared, her mouth wide open. She picked up a few pieces. "They're all on hangers yet? Why didn't she keep her hangers? These are store-bought ones not the free ones from a dry cleaner."

Matt had also noticed the hangers. He saw that Evelyn had a certain amount of trepidation in her voice.

"A man dropped them off this time."

Evelyn looked up at him with a confused look on her face. Matt just shrugged and pushed the cart to the check-in station for Evelyn to unload, check and sort.

Evelyn started processing the clothes immediately. She loved to create stories about gowns dropped off, about the special events they had seen, and the clothes from the lady in the Mercedes always generated lots of thought play. Matt stood by a few minutes to enjoy her intrigue.

"Oh my." Evelyn couldn't help it. This was a very unusual group of clothing. "This is unbelievable. Look at this. Hairpins, socks, oh my goodness. I think this is the first time in all my years I've seen someone actually drop off underwear. And they're all folded neatly like they just came out of the drawer."

She turned to him. "Matt, This has to be the Mercedes woman's entire wardrobe, all of her personal stuff. What happened to her? Who dropped this stuff off?"

Evelyn didn't stop talking long enough for Matt to respond. There was a story greater than an individual outfit. It was a real mystery. With a tone of certainty and some sadness, Evelyn said, "Mrs. M. must have died."

Matt had not been relieved from his post at the door, but he couldn't help himself. He started helping Evelyn sort through the bin. He was still close enough to the drop-off door to hear if a car drove up.

"It was a man in his fifties, but he drove her car. Now that I think about it, he might have looked a little sad. Maybe he hit a mid-life crisis and traded his wife in for a younger model." Matt gave Evelyn a mischievious grin along with his outlandish story.

Evelyn rolled her eyes at him. "You always think the worst of people, don't you? The woman must have passed away. If he had a girlfriend, it'd have been his clothing here, not the wife's. She'd have taken all this with her when she left and given away *his* things."

This made sense to Matt, but he wasn't to be outdone. "Maybe he *murdered* his wife." He was just being antagonistic. "Yes, that's it, and he had to remove all sign of her from the house."

Again Evelyn rolled her eyes and added a shake of her head. "Like we don't keep records? Murderers don't give away their victims' stuff to Goodwill."

Matt knew he was out of Evelyn's league. Fortunately, he heard another car drive up and headed outside.

Evelyn continued to go through Mrs. M.'s possessions, piece by piece. Lots of times clothing that came in had to be discarded because it was too worn or dirty. None of Mrs. M.'s things needed to be thrown away. Everything was in beautiful condition and very modern. Most of it was in season.

Evelyn had already surmised that Mrs. M. changed most of her wardrobe each season. She only kept a few transitional pieces. It was fun to sort through such fine clothing and see how the other half lived. The more she sorted, the more the clothing called to Evelyn. Finally, she seemed possessed by the need to find out what really happened to Mrs. M.

Evelyn had all of the pieces hung up by the next time Matt came in from outside. Matt glanced around at the racks.

"Mrs. M. must have a huge closet," he remarked.

"Some of the pieces were folded like they were stored in drawers. I hung those up too, of course. Look at all these pieces. I wonder if she wore an outfit more than twice?"

"Or at all?" Matt said as he pulled out the store tag still on a piece of clothing.

"I've found several like that. You're going to laugh at me. But I feel like the clothes are calling for me to find the truth. What happened to Mrs. M.? One person's life shouldn't be so easy to dispose of, should it? It's been reduced to the clothing and personal items dropped off at Goodwill. That's so very sad, isn't it?"

"I thought sorting this would cheer you up. I thing it's making you sadder. Tell me about what you've found. It's slow outside, so we've got some time." Matt was standing where he could see people driving up into the drop off area.

Evelyn grabbed hold of the shoulders of several items. "These clothes have a story to tell." Evelyn went to one of the racks she had filled. She removed a tuxedo with an accessories bag attached to the hanger. Then she showed Matt three formal dresses. "Look at this tuxedo. It's the only man's outfit amidst all of the women's clothing. It has matching accessories to these three gowns."

"And look at these formal gowns. They're timeless beauties." Evelyn held up each of the dresses individually. The first dress was pale green with forest green trimmings. The second dress was a soft shade of pink with a burgundy sash and burgundy decorative stitching. The third gown was a soft, iridescent blue so pale that it looked like a blue light was reflecting off a white gown.

To dramatize her point, Evelyn laid each dress across the table and took the accessories of the tuxedo. The cummerbunds came in forest green, burgundy, and dark blue. Evelyn laid them over the gowns.

"These were purchased for a very specific purpose because each dress has matching tuxedo accessories. I'd guess that she wore the dresses multiple times because they're classic styles. Sentimental memories go with these outfits."

Matt smirked. "What makes you think that?"

"Most of the rest of her wardrobe was changed each season. These she kept from year to year. They even invested money so his tuxedo had accent colors to her dress."

"That's a very interesting theory," Matt said, then grinned. "Do you have a story created for the outfits?"

"Not today. There's a larger, sadder story that needs to be discovered first. I'm going to find out what happened to Mrs. M. So, Mr. Manager are you done filling in at receiving?"

Matt glanced at his watch, although he could see the regular employee coming back from break.

"Yup. I'm back to manager responsibilities."

"Good. I've got a special request."

Matt narrowed his eyes. "Why do I feel like I'm going to regret saying this? What is it?"

"Can we put the tuxedo and accessories together with the three dresses for a sales group?"

"You know that's strictly against policy."

As Matt said that, Evelyn looked at him with forlorn pleading. He was such a sucker for that look, and she knew not to over use it.

"Oh, okay. Put the set at $28.95, but they'll still need to be individually marked. You can tag them as a matching ensemble. But once one piece in the set is sold, they get hung with their normal groupings. If they aren't sold hanging together within three weeks, then they'll get moved into the separate locations. Deal?" Matt knew that Evelyn would be doing everything she could to influence the sale of these items together.

"Deal. Thanks, Matt."

Evelyn smiled and began the marking process. She figured a greater amount for the tuxedo with accessories and an equal amount for each of the three dresses. The total came to $28.95 as directed. It was times like these that she wished that she could work all the time. Evelyn wanted, no, needed, to know who brought this batch of clothes into the store. She also needed to know who might purchase them. This elegant set was calling her. She told herself that, this time, the story she formulated about the clothing was going to be real and not just one of her fantasies. Evelyn had a feeling that the truth was going to be stranger and more wonderful than fiction.

2

Okay, the wedding list and budget," Joan said to herself, picking up her carefully itemized sheets of legal paper.

"Oh!" she let out an exasperated sigh. "There are times I wish either of our families had more money than they do. I do get jealous of those girls whose families take out big loans for their weddings," she added not really wanting to see her family strapped just to please her.

Joan reviewed the list one more time. "The professional photographer's been scheduled, and the money is in the savings for that." This made her smile. "The rings have been paid in full." Then she looked at the rest of the list and she sighed. The meal, soloist, pastor, decorations, flowers, honeymoon, a suit for Jeremy and dress for her, bridesmaids dresses—"This list is never ending."

Joan placed her left hand on her forehead and leaned on it as she stared at the overwhelming expense of the most modest of wedding dresses. She was glad that her internship at Manufacturing Plus had turned into a full-time job. She and Jeremy had been able to save more than what they were expecting, but it was still far from covering the list of expenses.

"Okay, focus," she told herself firmly. She needed to set up a time to meet with Theresa to pick out the silk flowers. Theresa had a store discount that would save them a great deal. But they only had about $200 reserved for Jeremy's suit and her wedding dress. That was going to be very tight—nigh impossible from the prices she'd been seeing. She knew she needed to get the wedding clothes purchased before she firmed up some of the other things. Then there was food for over a hundred people. They had already cut their list in half, but still that many people were going to be overwhelming to feed.

Joan's mind began to wander. She remembered the day she and Jeremy had taken a country drive and seen a tiny country church. The beautiful stained-glass windows had caught both of their eyes. Amazingly, the congregation had been outside doing spring cleaning just as they drove by. It was just like God had directed them to turn into that driveway. The people were so friendly and the woodwork inside was absolutely beautiful. Joan had never seen woodwork that ornate, especially in a church that seated only about a hundred fifty people."

The reception could be somewhere else, but the members assured them that the tiny basement kitchen and reception area would work wonderfully. The little country church made the perfect wedding chapel. "Too bad it doesn't fit more people," Joan mused. "They could make some real money."

Joan looked over the invitation list, and the thought occurred that they should have just eloped.

Joan jumped as the phone rang. "Hello."

"How is the most beautiful woman in the world doing today?"

Joan smiled when she heard Jeremy's voice. "Panicking. The wedding's two months away, and I haven't found a gown yet. And we don't have a suit for you either. I just haven't been able to find anything in my size that comes anywhere near the budget," Joan said in frustration.

"We've been praying hard that you'll find something nice. Remember, I don't care if it's a formal white gown or just a nice dress. In fact, that dress you picked up for Joy's wedding would be nice," Jeremy said.

Men, thought Joan. Maybe it didn't have to be a formal wedding dress, but it did have to be special. "I'm going to keep looking. I usually use my day off to go to the second-hand stores and sales. Do you want to join me today?"

"I'll be right over," Jeremy said.

He arrived in record time. Joan looked nervous. "Before we go, let's pray. Lord, take this burden from us."

Jeremy added, "Let us find today that perfect dress that you have for her and a suit for me."

"Jeremy, you're so funny," Joan said sarcastically.

"But God cares about all our worries."

Joan rolled her eyes at Jeremy's statement, even though she had been praying for the same thing if only to herself. But it did sound a bit strange to hear the words come out.

They drove together on the way to all three second-hand stores in town. "Maybe it's time we start going to the specialty stores," Jeremy said. "Some girls I've worked with purchased inexpensive gowns that had been tried on several times or used in bridal shows but never actually worn."

Joan shrugged and continued to go over the wedding details as they drove. "The reception's all set. Amy and her mother are making the cakes. I had formally asked her mother to do them. She told me it was going to be our wedding present from them. Sandy and her mom are going to make the salad. We just need to buy the groceries for them. We need to make up a hundred ham sandwiches on buns—"

"Wait a minute," Jeremy interrupted her. "Why only a hundred? We've got more guests than that coming and some people will eat more than one sandwich."

Joan nodded. "A group of women in another department at work heard about my wedding plans. They were impressed that we're trying to keep costs low. Someone told them about the things we're planning and that it's 'cash or no go.' As they headed back from their break to work, they stopped by my work station and gave me a list of their names and home phone numbers. They told me they wanted to work the reception for me so I could save more money."

Jeremy gaped. "Are you kidding?"

"Nope. In fact, when I called them at home and gave them the menu, they told me they'd like to bring the punch. Then they said that, if we could make a hundred sandwiches, they'd make the rest. They also suggested that we put chairs in circles instead of sitting at tables."

"That's an option we've been discussing."

Joan nodded again. "If we greet the guests row by row as we dismiss them, they can go straight into the reception in small groups. The wedding party'll already be sitting in various spots around the room. Many people will be done eating by the time we get into the reception area and begin mingling."

"I'll need to think about that." He pulled into a parking lot. "Here we are. Let the shopping begin." Jeremy didn't like shopping really, but he loved spending time with Joan and knew it was important to her for him to be supportive.

"Jeremy, you can't see my gown until you see me walking down the aisle at the church," Joan teased.

"Then I'll close my eyes when I look," Jeremy teased back. "Does the same go for what the groom wears?"

"Hmmm. No. And that's a good thing because you'd buy the first thing you saw."

They were in and out of the first two stores fairly quickly. There wasn't anything new. When they went through the formal rack at the Goodwill store, there were a few new things, but nothing appropriate for a wedding.

Evelyn was working nearby and overhead their conversation, easily perking her ears when she heard "wedding."

"Well, Jeremy, sorry to drag you out for nothing. I thought we'd at least be able to find a suit for you to wear to the wedding. I wish we could afford a tuxedo."

"Joan, you promised that we'd check out the bridal shops to see if they had anything discounted. Don't give up yet."

"Excuse me," Evelyn said. "I don't mean to be eavesdropping, but are you really looking for a tuxedo?"

"Well, a tux would be nice, but we were actually looking for a nice suit. But if there's a tuxedo, that'd be wonderful. I'm also looking for a bridal gown," Joan replied.

Evelyn smiled. She took Joan's hand and led her to a special rack. "We got this set in earlier this week. We kept it together as a set, so it isn't in with the rest of the formal clothing. The tuxedo's in excellent shape, and this matching iridescent-blue dress almost looks like it's white reflecting a blue light. Let me show it to you," Evelyn said as she walked them over to the mirror and held up the tuxedo and dress in front of them for effect.

Joan looked for a tag to see the size. But the dress didn't have a tag. It was handmade by an expert seamstress. The material was beautiful.

"This looks like my size and it's pretty. I'm going to try it on," Joan said as she headed into the fitting room with the blue dress. Evelyn knew she wasn't supposed to be spending time with customers as a private shopper, but, she couldn't resist with this couple.

"Sir, why don't you try this on?" Evelyn handed Jeremy the matching tuxedo.

Joan walked out, but Jeremy was nowhere to be found. Evelyn was waiting for her, however.

"Oh, that looks beautiful on you. And it fits absolutely perfectly. I sent your fiancé into the other dressing room with the tuxedo."

Just then Jeremy came out. He was fighting with the cummerbund, and the tie was in his hand. Evelyn took charge and helped him. Then she stood them side by side in front of the three-fold mirrors. Joan and Jeremy stared in disbelief. Then their smiles grew.

"Jeremy, this is perfect."

"I agree and to make it even better, they are being sold as a set," Jeremy repeated what Evelyn had told him.

"These two dresses also go with the set," Evelyn told them. "Everything for $28.95."

"Even if they don't work for Sandy and Amy, you can't go wrong with the price," Jeremy said.

"They are both about a size smaller than I am, but Sandy's mom can do alterations. We'll take them," Joan said excitedly. Then she and Jeremy changed back into their street clothes and checked out. Two thirds of their bridal party was going to be dressed for only $28.95. Suddenly their finances were stretching to fit their wedding. The groomsmen still needed to rent tuxedos, but that wasn't their expense. "Do you think the guys're going to be upset that we're going to make them rent tuxedos now?" Joan whispered to Jeremy.

"No. Neither of them owns a suit. So it'll be fine."

Evelyn hovered at the end of check-out. "Can you do me a favor and drop me off a wedding photo? If you don't see me here, you can give it to the manager on duty." Evelyn had grown shy, but she made a point of asking them this. It was the truth calling to her, waiting to be told, and she had the feeling she would need to draw it full circle before this was over.

"We'll do that," Joan said with a big smile. She wanted to hug this woman for pointing them towards the dresses. "The wedding's two months away yet. But we'll be in after that."

EARLIER MATT HAD BEEN WATCHING Evelyn and the couple from a distance. He knew Evelyn. She was very careful with the store rules. He watched with a smile when the couple was looking at the special set Evelyn had begged to set aside.

Matt had assumed that Evelyn would create a story about the life of the outfits before they arrived. Then she'd take the photo of the wedding and complete her fairytale. The Mercedes drop off hadn't lifted Evelyn's spirits as quickly as Matt had hoped it would, but today he was seeing the payoff. She looked transfixed.

What he missed seeing was the calling Mrs. M.'s drop off had to Evelyn. It had started a fire burning deep within her spirit, a fire that was not going to be easily quenched.

℘ 3 ☙

I SEE YOUR SECOND-HAND TUXEDO ensemble sold," Matt said casually to Evelyn the next day.

"Yes, to a wonderful young couple. It's going to be used for their wedding in about two months," Evelyn said with a smug smile.

"Did they promise a photo?"

"They did. I hope they remember."

"Found out anything about the mystery of Mrs. M. yet?"

"I'm pleased to announce that no one's been reported missing or murdered."

"Darn, I was hoping for an exciting conclusion," Matt said with his version of a sinister look. "What've you found out about the other theories?"

"I went to the local newspaper, online, for the last month. There was nothing in the obituaries and nothing in the social pages. I'm going to keep watching. I've gotta know about this one. I'm going to dig deeper than normal. My friend Travis might be able to help me track down the Mercedes. Do you remember the numbers on the plates?"

Matt shrugged. "They were personalized. Almost like a phrase. But I couldn't figure it out. I always tell myself I'm going to remember them until I figured it out." Matt had stepped out of the conversation and was now talking to himself. "It doesn't help. I forget anyway." Matt paused when he realized that he was thinking out loud. He looked up at Evelyn and said, "Let me think about it for a while. I'll see if I can remember anything."

"I knew it was a long shot." Evelyn paused. She had never let her curiosity take her this far before. "I know this is a dangerous request but can I view the security tapes from the time of the drop off?"

Matt raised an eyebrow. "This is more than your normal game. Security tapes to identify the Mercedes? That's pretty serious." He smiled. Evelyn's fire had been ignited. He was going to do everything to fuel the flame.

"I can't explain why but I need to know more."

"Let me make a few phone calls and see if I can get permission. I can't promise anything," Matt said. Then he headed towards his office to see what he could do. He had to do this for Evelyn. He turned back towards her and said, "You never make unusual requests. And I'd like to see you have a third story published in *Reader's Digest*."

Evelyn went back to work. She was making mental notes each time one of Mrs. M.'s outfits sold. *These aren't really difficult to track. Mrs. M.'s clothing is more expensive than the clothing normally donated*, she thought to herself as she straightened an area with several pieces of Mrs. M.'s clothing. Each piece that sold made her desire to solve the mystery of Mrs. M. grow deeper.

"The word is out—here come the vultures." The group of women walking into the store caught Evelyn's attention. "Come to think of it, I've been seeing women from all social classes purchasing Mrs. M.'s clothing." Evelyn watched as the women found several pieces. They were all very excited about the purchases they were making. The women who ferreted out the pieces with store tags still on them acted like they had gold in their hands. They were purchasing name brand items for less than five dollars, never used.

I wish Matt would say something about the security tapes, Evelyn thought as she moved away to another area of the store. *I'm afraid he's been told no and doesn't know how to tell me. I've hit dead ends everywhere else. My investigation is at a stand still. I guess I'm not as good a detective as I thought.* Each dead end she hit made her more determined to solve the mystery around Mrs. M. Evelyn's thoughts were interrupted when she heard someone coming.

"Evelyn. What are you doing this weekend?"

"I thought I'd spend a couple of days looking through society pages. Maybe I'll get lucky and see some of Mrs. M.'s clothing on a woman. If I do, I'll print the photos out and test your memory."

"This might help you out." Matt handed Evelyn a computer disk. "I couldn't get permission for you to view the tapes. But I've got security to view them and make a disc. I couldn't do it during working hours, though. So, I stayed a couple of hours after until I found what's on this disc. By the way, you owe my wife. She wants to hear the story that you create when you've solved your mystery."

"I hope it's a story I can tell. Thanks for this. Do I 'not know' where this came from?" It was a strange question but one Evelyn often asked as she did research.

"How about the 'don't ask, don't tell' policy," Matt said with an innocent smile.

"In other words, don't spread it around, but I can tell the truth if asked?" Evelyn clarified. Matt was still smiling. He winked at her as he walked away.

Evelyn couldn't wait to go home and check out what was on the disk. She hoped to see a picture of the car, maybe the driver. Most of all she wanted to see the license plate. The hope that she had been losing at each dead end was rekindled with this new lead.

ꕥ 4 ꕥ

AMY AND SANDY MET AT JOAN'S on Saturday morning to try on the dresses. Joan was right, they both needed minor alterations.

"You spent $28.95 all together? Really? Let's see yours!" Amy said excitedly. Joan quickly changed into her dress.

"It's awesome!" Sandy squealed. "And a perfect fit. If all the dresses fit you it would be a shame to alter them so they don't."

"When would I ever wear them? Especially for what I paid for them, I'd rather have them altered and used for the wedding. Besides the bouquets are on the agenda today. I have the colored ties that match your dresses. We'll take them to the discount flower warehouse and see what we can find that matches." Joan tucked the ties she had been holding up into her purse.

"Let's drop the dresses off with Mom before we go shopping," Sandy suggested. "She'll need to see them on us so it doesn't pay to change."

"You just want to prance around in a formal." Joan pretended to strut obnoxiously around the room.

Her gown didn't need any alterations. "I'll quick change. Sandy, Amy, stop your prancing and gather your clothes together."

Sandy and Amy, who had copied Joan in strutting around the room, were acting like they were famous models doing a runway show.

"Yes, ma'am. She sure is bossy today," Amy said with overly exaggerated gestures.

"Don't worry. Payback, you know," Sandy added as they picked up their clothing. They had the last piece gathered together when Joan came back.

"Let's go. We have a big day ahead of us. Saving money takes time," Joan said with a laugh. That was all it took, and they laughed and giggled about everything all the way to Sandy's house.

"Hello, girls, you look pretty. Are you all dressed up with nowhere to go?" Sandy's mom teased. It wasn't that funny, but the three girls broke out into a fit of giggles anyway. Then they slowly twirled in front of Sandy's mom. Everyone was afraid to say a word for fear they would break out into giggles again.

Sandy's mom knew these three girls well enough to finish the fittings in silence. Neither dress was going to need much for alterations. She would have them finished before the girls finished making the bouquets.

"May I speak without you girls breaking out into a giggle fit?"

Joan, Sandy and Amy looked Sandy's mom straight in the eyes and pressed their lips together. They were the most ridiculous looking threesome she'd ever seen.

"I'll be done with these this evening. Why don't you bring shoes, bouquets, and Joan's dress over here for supper? We'll have a final fitting. Just nod your heads." The three girls nodded. "See you at five o'clock. Now, change and go."

As soon as they were out of sight, they began giggling again. Sandy's mom just shook her head. There were times she wondered if any of these three would ever be mature enough to be married.

Within minutes the girls were laying dresses on the table beside Sandy's mom. Then they ran out the door. They were on a mission now, and nothing was going to stop them.

Sandy called her friend, Theresa, on the way to the floral warehouse. Theresa, who had her own items to buy there, was going to guide the three of them to what they needed to purchase.

"Theresa, thanks so much for helping us," Sandy said as they met her at the store entrance.

"You're welcome. Do you have any ideas for flowers yet?"

"Here are the accent colors of the bridesmaids' dresses. We hope the bouquets will match both the men's tuxedos and the dresses." Joan pulled out the colored ties from her purse.

"Excellent colors to work with. We could find flowers for three stand-alone bouquets."

"Huh?" Joan was lost. "Yes, each of us is going to have a separate bouquet except when the maid of honor holds mine, then she'll have two."

"No, no. I mean each person would carry a uniquely color bouquet."

"Oh, I got it now. No, I thought we'd tie the bridal party together by mixing the three accent colors into similar bouquets. My dress is white with an iridescent blue shimmer to it. I'm not sure about holding a bouquet that's completely white. Do you have any suggestions?"

"Hmmm." Theresa thought for a minute. "Okay, I have an idea for that. Did you make a list of people who'll have bouquets, corsages, or boutonnières?"

"Yup. Here it is. I thought traditional red for this group." Joan pointed to the parents, grandparents, and honored guests.

Theresa put Joan's list next to her own, and they both took carts. Joan, Sandy, and Amy followed along behind Theresa. Without saying much about what she was purchasing, Theresa started dumping things into Joan's cart.

After a tour around the store, both carts were full. "I'll write out one check and you can pay me when we get back to your place." Everyone except Theresa seemed to be overwhelmed. "Don't worry. I'll get you going."

Theresa got a subtotal between the two carts so they could keep their expenses separate. Theresa often shopped for multiple projects with subtotals in between. It wasn't an unusual request. Joan's items were rung up first, then the rest of Theresa's items.

"Sandy, I left the directions to Joan's at home. Can you write them down for me again?" Theresa had lost track of time and had run too quickly out of her place that morning.

"I'll just ride with you." Sandy did not like giving directions.

The two cars followed each other back to Joan's place. They quickly unloaded Joan's supplies for the bouquets.

"Good, your kitchen table is clear. Gals, dump your bags out across the table," Theresa instructed. "First, we'll sort by groupings. Bouquet flowers over here. Corsage colors there, and the supplies to put them together in the center."

Theresa gave her instructions as basically as she could so that the other three wouldn't get confused. She had about an hour to get them going before she had to be on her way. She pulled out Joan's list then decided that Sandy would do the corsages, Amy the boutonnières, and Joan the bouquets.

"Amy, you first. I'll show you how to make the boutonnières for the men. I'll make the one for the groom while you make your first one." Theresa grouped together the supplies they would each need for the first two. Then she walked Amy through the process step by step. The groom's had twice the flowers and Theresa finished well before Amy was done.

"Looks good, Amy. Cut a piece of paper, write the name on it and pin it to the bottom of the flower like this. Now pull out what you need for the next one and work on that one while I show Sandy the corsages." Theresa followed the same steps with Sandy. The first two were complete, and Sandy continued on to the other names on her list.

"Joan, it's your turn now. I'll do your bouquet while you do one of the others. You talked about wanting your bouquet to have a train. Our goal is that I work down the train and you do the second matching bouquet. You'll be done before Sandy and Amy."

"That's the way it should be."

For all their giggling earlier, the girls were all so deep in concentration about what they were doing that the conversation had dropped down to almost nothing.

"Theresa, that's a perfect color combination and design. Wow, I can't believe from my scattered ideas how you pulled the perfect bouquet together," Joan stated.

Each of the bridesmaids had an open white rose in the center with a combination of dark blue flowers and burgundy roses surrounding it. Theresa had found the perfect forest-green folliage. A small amount of baby's breath broke up the darkness around the edges, and they had found lace in all three colors. Each bouquet had its unique color for the lace.

The bride's bouquet had an open white rose in the center and white roses blended in with burgundy roses and blue flowers. Theresa formed a train with the greenery for her bouquet, giving it extra length. Then she tied a variety of the flowers including baby's breath into the train.

When she was done, she stepped into the other room with the bridal bouquet. Hearing the *sht, sht* sound of a spray can, the three girls stopped working. They looked at each other with confusion and curiosity.

"Theresa?" Joan called out.

Theresa popped her head back into the room with a smile on her face. "Yes? Did you run into a problem?"

"No. What are you up to?" Joan asked as she closed one eye and scrunched her face the way she did when she was thinking hard.

"Finishing touches. Close your eyes. All of you," Theresa replied as she returned to the room. All three closed their eyes. Theresa took the bouquet and passed it under each of their noses.

"It smells like real roses," Joan said as she opened her eyes. "Wow, that's so sweet."

"I brought a flower bag and box. Spray the flowers then let them dry. When they're dry, put them in the bag. You may need to spray them again a week before the wedding. Just don't overdo it. You want them to smell real not putrid."

Joan thanked Theresa for her help as Theresa ran out the door. Sandy and Amy still had about an hour of work left to do. Joan was amazed at how professional everything was turning out.

ꙮ 5 ꙮ

EVELYN SIGNED ONTO HER COMPUTER as soon as she got home. The program started up, allowing her to look at Matt's information.

"You've got to be kidding." Evelyn had a habit of talking to herself when she did computer research. "The best shot of Mr. M. is the back of his head. And the two shots of the plate are so blurry I can't tell the letters from the numbers." Despite feeling like she didn't have anything good to work with, she decided to call her friend Travis.

"Hello, Travis."

"Evelyn. Did you get the information on that plate?"

"Yes and No. I've got a couple of photos, but they're so blurry I can't read them."

"I'm off work for the weekend. Why don't you bring over what you've got, and we'll see what we can do."

"I haven't eaten supper yet, have you?"

"No."

"How does pizza sound?"

"Sounds good. I'm not picky."

"Okay, I'll pick one up on the way over. See you soon." Evelyn hung up, then called in a pizza order to the shop just down the road from Travis's place. She knew it was his favorite pizza place. Travis loved thick, chewy crusts and five cheeses. She knew the difficulty of the task she was going to ask him to do and wanted to come in loaded with the best bribe she could think of giving him. Thirty minutes later, Evelyn was pulling up in front of Travis's place.

"Ooh. Pizza from Grandpa Peretti's Pizza Parlor. My favorite!" Travis said as he opened the door. Then he scrutinized her. "Is it really that bad of a photo?"

"I'll let you judge that for yourself. But I'm starved, so I vote that we dig into this pizza while it is still hot."

"Yeah, the smell of Papa's Italian seasonings is making me drool."

Travis was like a son to Evelyn. Despite the generation gap, they related well to each other. They were both respectful of the other. This project was going to stretch that relationship to its limit.

Travis stuck the last piece of pizza into his mouth and, talking with his mouth full, mumbled, "Let's go into the den." He took the disk Evelyn handed him and downloaded the information into his computer. The fuzzy photos came up quickly.

"I think that the store needs to update this security system," Travis said. He gave Evelyn a look that confirmed her suspicion. Travis was going to need a miracle to figure out the license plate.

"Is there any hope at all?" Evelyn knew this shouldn't be as important as it was to her. But the more dead ends she hit, the more she needed to know about Mr. and Mrs. M.

"There's always hope. I'll give it my best try. Let's work together on it for a while." Travis could tell that this was important to Evelyn.

Evelyn pulled up a chair beside Travis as he loaded the photos into an experimental clarification program he had. He hadn't been too impressed with the results in the past. But it was his best shot at home.

First, he cropped the photos so that they would only look at the license plate. With the cropped photos loaded, he processed each one and saved it to a new file name. It took about five minutes for the photos to process. He repeated the processing procedure several times. It didn't help. It wasn't making any discernable difference.

"It's okay, Travis. I knew it was a long shot. The tape was just too poor to get anything clear from it," Evelyn said in a defeatist tone.

"Don't give up yet. Some local FBI officers were at work a few weeks ago. One of them was collecting information on cold cases they were going to take into a classroom setting and challenge the trainees to review and solve."

"What? That's wicked. Giving trainees an unsolvable case to solve that the pros couldn't?"

"Actually, having fresh eyes look at a case without preconceived ideas often helps. They'll see things that are so obvious that seasoned officers tend to miss them.

Anyway, he left me his card in case I came across anything interesting. Let me see if I can get him to bite. Maybe the trainees can help you solve your case."

"Do they have access to actual data bases?"

"Yes, actually they do. Let's draw this up like a missing person. Do you have your notebook so we can go over some of your notes?"

"I left it in the car. I'll go get it." Evelyn retrieved her notebook. They put together what little bits of information they had regarding Mr. and Mrs. Mercedes. "I have a bit of a concern."

"What's that?"

"If they find Mr. M., he won't actually be detained and questioned, will he?" Evelyn asked very naively.

"If, in their research, they find that it really is a missing person's case, he may be. But I'll let the instructor know that it's not really a missing person, more an exercise. Do you have one of your stories with you? I can send it along and let him know that the information will be used as research for your next story."

"Do you still have the copy of the *Reader's Digest* that I gave you last month?"

"Oh, that's right. I'll get that and make a copy of it. From an official publication, it'll mean even more to the instructor. This could take a while, but it's our best chance. I'll let you know what he says."

"Thanks, Travis. The other half of the story, the wedding that the tuxedo and dresses were purchased for is still over a month away."

"But that doesn't diminish your curiosity does it?" He smiled knowingly.

Evelyn just smiled. Travis knew her very well. It was going to be a difficult wait for her. The burning desire to know was continuing to build by the minute.

"I'll call you as soon as I'm able to get hold of the agent, and I'll keep you informed every step of the way." Travis paused a second as he walked Evelyn to the door. "Drive home safely."

"I always do," She replied. As she turned and left, she thought to herself, *Another twist in the path. The suspense is killing me, but I love it.* Evelyn's smile grew as she walked out to her car. There was still hope.

6

JOAN WAS LOOKING OVER HER LIST of to-do items for the wedding. A couple of weeks had passed since the weekend the girls had made the flowers. Everything was in order for the wedding. Joan was surprised at how relieved she had been when the dresses were purchased and fitted and the flowers were complete. Other than the decorating and reception work, all the other things left undone were incidentals. If they didn't get worked out, no one else would notice.

"Hello, I'm looking for the most beautiful woman in the world. Have I found her?" Jeremy said when Joan answered the phone.

"Since we're talking on the phone, I could tell you anything, and you'd have to believe me," Joan teased back. "What've you been up to today?"

"Nothing too exciting. I just haven't told you that I love you for twenty-four hours, and I thought you needed to hear that."

"When we're old and gray and can barely hear each other, I'll never be offended by you yelling that to me. I love you, too. I've been missing you."

"Not for long. The wedding's getting closer. Until then, how about a romantic date?"

"Sounds good. What were you thinking about?"

"There are several travel agencies in town. Let's go visit all of them and see if we can find a special deal for our honeymoon. Then we can go out for supper afterwards and discuss the possibilities."

"You certainly have high expectations, don't you?" Joan knew they only had about three hundred dollars to spend on the honeymoon.

"God provided my tuxedo, your dress, and the bridesmaids dresses for a fraction of the amount you were expecting to spend. That doubles our honeymoon money, and maybe now we can do more than just a weekend at a nearby hotel. We won't know unless we check it out." Jeremy was tempting Joan. She had been trying not to get her hopes up too high.

"I know that God can provide anything. Part of my problem is that I don't even know what to ask for because I don't know where I want to go." Joan was being honest. Because they didn't have much money for the honeymoon, she hadn't taken the time to dream of possibilities like most brides-to-be.

"I guess it sounds like a date then. Can you be ready in half an hour?"

"If I'm not, you'll just have to wait for me," Joan said with a smile. Jeremy hated waiting and he was always pushing to get going before Joan or any reasonable woman could be ready.

Jeremy was over in twenty minutes. Joan looked at the clock as she answered the door. She wasn't close to being ready. She split the time and took an additional twenty minutes so that she was only ten minutes late to his ten minutes early.

Jeremy knew better than to arrive too early. When they set a time, that was the time Joan expected him. If he was five minutes early, she always managed to be five minutes late. One time he tested his theory. He sat in his car until the exact minute by his clock and walked up to the door. She was ready on time.

He wondered how, once they were married, this would change. Jeremy was hoping that, if they set a time to leave and he refrained from saying, "Are you ready" or "Let's go" before the designated time, she would be ready on time. For today, he didn't mind spending the extra twenty minutes in her company as she got ready.

"Now I'm ready to go!" Joan announced as she walked into the kitchen for the fourth time.

"Sounds wonderful. Let's pray before we leave. Lord, Thank you for blessing us with extra money for our honeymoon. Please give us wisdom and blessings as we look for a vacation that'll be fun and memorable. Amen," Jeremy ended with confidence.

"I'm going to pick up the mail as we head out," Joan said casually. "The RSVP cards have started coming back in the mail." Joan opened the mailbox, and there was a pile of her small RSVP envelopes and one larger envelope. She slid open the card.

"Look. We got our first wedding card."

"Who's it from?" Jeremy said as he held the door open, prompting her through it. Joan followed as she focused on the card.

"It's from the Westons. My bosses all through high school." She stopped talking a second as she read their personal note. All of a sudden the RSVP notes started slipping out of her hands. There wasn't much of a breeze, but Jeremy leaned over and quickly picked up what she had dropped.

"What is it? What's wrong?"

"Nothing. Listen to this note."

"Joan and Jeremy,

Congratulations on your impending wedding. We regret that we will not be able to attend. Joan, it was such a pleasure to have you as an employee for all those years. You were unlike any other employee we had in the past or have had since. We knew that you were working to help out with your family's bills when the other teens worked for fun money. We have talked it over and decided to bless you in a special way. Please use this money towards your honeymoon."

"I don't believe this. Jeremy sit down before I show you this." Jeremy had been holding the car door open for Joan, who was now seated in the passenger seat. He closed the door, walked around the car, got in, and sat down in the driver's seat. Then Joan passed the enclosed check to Jeremy. There were tears in her eyes.

"Wow! This is incredible," Jeremy gasped. "This is a thousand dollars! Can that be right?"

"You prayed for it. Why don't you believe it?" Joan gave him a puzzled look.

"I guess I was expecting to find a good deal on a trip, not to get an extra thousand to spend. I'm not complaining. I'm just surprised."

"Let's go," Joan stated as she took the check from him and wrote up a deposit slip. "I've got a detour. Bank first to deposit this check, *then* we begin looking."

Going into the travel agencies with almost sixteen hundred dollars made the experience a little less stressful. It opened up their options significantly. "I guess we'll be able to fly further than Las Vegas," Jeremy said. It was the only trip either of them had found for their initial amount, a two-day round trip to Las Vegas.

Joan and Jeremy walked into their first travel agency. "Hello, We are planning our honeymoon. Is there someone who can help us?"

"Certainly, where are you thinking of going?" the agent inquired.

"That's part of the problem. We really have no idea where we want to go," Jeremy said as he noticed the frustration building on the agent's face.

"And we only have $1,600 to spend, including incidentals," Joan stated apologetically.

"Well, I can give you some general ideas. The prices go up and down the closer it gets to when you leave. If you see something you like that's within your budget, I'd recommend that you lock into it right away."

They left the agency with several brochures. It was the same thing at each of the other agencies. If they weren't really picky, some of the trips just over their budget might come down if they waited a couple of days. Cancun was almost within their reach.

"Jeremy, I'm on overload. There are too many choices." Joan sounded exhausted as they drove to the restaurant.

"I know what you mean. Visiting that third place put me over the top, too. Did you get good notes at each place?"

"We'll see when we get inside. I think I did. But sometimes when I get overwhelmed, I can't read my own writing." Joan looked over at Jeremy with a lost look on her face.

"Let's go inside, order a great meal and start dreaming a little bit." Jeremy opened the car door for Joan. She was sitting there, still overwhelmed by all of the information racing through her head. Jeremy placed his hand on her shoulder, and she jumped. "I didn't mean to startle you, Sweetie, but we're here. Hand me the notebook and brochures, and let's go inside."

Joan handed Jeremy the information then slowly got out of the car. She inhaled deeply, "Have you ever noticed that it always smells like charbroiled steaks here?" She commented.

Jeremy had chosen an affordable restaurant in town for their date. They had arrived before the normal supper rush, and there was plenty of privacy.

When asked the number of their party, Jeremy answered, "Only two, but if we may, we'd like a larger booth, please." Joan and Jeremy recognized many of the people on staff. This was their favorite restaurant.

"Follow me." The hostess directed them to a large corner booth that normally seated six people. "How's this?"

"Wonderful! Thank-you." Joan slid around first then Jeremy slid close to her. They took a quick minute to decide what they wanted. They looked at the menus even though they knew them by memory.

"Hello, I'm Carol, and I'll be your server today. Can I get you something to drink while you decide?" Carol was new and was still very formal with them.

"No, we've decided already. We're both going to have the steak and egg breakfast. Mine with the steak well done and the eggs over easy, and Joan's with the steak medium and the eggs over soft. Orange juice for both of us and a pitcher of water."

"Over soft?"

"Who's cooking today? Kevin?" Joan asked Carol.

"Yes."

"Kevin will understand what I mean by over soft." Joan smiled trying to reassure the waitress. Kevin had a way of sprinkling water around her egg and covering it so that it steam cooked in the same time that Jeremy's cooked.

Carol read back the order to them. After they confirmed that she had it right, she left. Joan and Jeremy immediately began sorting through the brochures.

"Jeremy, I'm glad you wrote the travel agency name on the brochures," Joan said as she sorted them into price groupings.

"What are our main choices?" Jeremy asked.

"Two to three days to the Riviera Mia just south of Cancun, Mexico, but the trip would need to lower in price for us to have any spending money. A Florida vacation with one day at Disneyland. New York City—two of the travel agencies had special bus tours going to New York," Joan said, recapping her notes.

For all of the options, they could afford the airfare or bus fare and hotel, but they would have very little spending money. As Jeremy and Joan looked at each other, the frustration melted into disappointment.

"Are you two planning your honeymoon?" Kathy, a waitress who knew them well, asked as she walked by their table.

"We're trying to. But we're totally overwhelmed. Some vacations are within our budget but need again that much for incidental spending. Others are just over but don't need any extra spending money. Of course the one we both seem to be drooling over, only one of us could afford to go," Joan said with an exasperated look on her face.

"My parents waited to the very last minute to book their cruise. Actually what they did was tell their travel agency that they needed thirty-six hours notice to pack, and the agent watched for a 'two for one' deal," Kathy offered.

"We have a time issue. We only have certain days off. But I suppose if we were open to taking whichever one and not knowing until the very last minute it would work."

All the waiters and waitresses they knew made their way by the table throughout the evening. They each added some input. They all knew that Jeremy and Joan believed in prayer. In the end, the advice given broke down into two groups. One group said to choose the one vacation they really wanted and pray for it. The other group thought they should leave it totally up to God. Pray for the best vacation available the Thursday before their wedding and lock in at the last minute. No matter what they decided, each one depended upon their prayers and God's direction.

Joan and Jeremy made their decision. They would pray about it.

7

THE MRS. M. CASE. I'm glad Travis brought this case to my attention. His timing was great, a week before class began." Mr. Thompkins, instructor of the crime investigation class, laid out five folders across his desk as he talked through the various cases.

"Cindy, Tara, and John have turned in preliminary reports. Then there's mine. I had to stay one step ahead of the students on this one," he said, smiling to himself. "Who am I kidding? Travis and Evelyn's report got me curious enough to join in. I could see Evelyn's desire to solve the question: what happened to Mrs. M.? She definitely put the packet together in an intriguing way. This is the first time in years I've looked forward to grading papers."

Mr. Thompkins reviewed each of the students' papers. Alone, they had done acceptable jobs. Now, he was going to throw a twist at them—teamwork.

"Can you help me take these reports to the classroom?" Mr. Thompkins asked his assistant, who had just walked into the room.

"Sure." Together they walked into the class with all the extra credit assignments ready for the students.

"Okay, everyone, take your seats. I've had a chance to look at all the individual preliminary findings for those who are doing the extra-credit projects. I've written teams on the board to the right. Please make a note of your team members. You'll finish this project as a team. Megan, please pass these back for me."

"What's our new deadline?" a student asked.

"Good question. It's been a month. I'll give you another month working together to find the solutions. All the groups will have a good starting point. But you'll need to work closely with each other to find the answers."

"Then you *do* know all of the answers." Cindy was trying to trick him into revealing a new tidbit she could work with.

"No, Cindy, I can assure you that I'll need to validate your final results. At this point, I've only looked at the information on your reports as if I were the one doing the investigation. I haven't marked any corrections on any of the reports."

"In other words, we could be totally wrong but using the right approach?" Cindy almost sounded depressed at the revelation.

All that she got from the instructor was a smile with a knowing point of his finger to his forehead. All of the teams groaned in unison.

The rest of the class time was spent in lecture. This was one class where no one minded the lecture portion. The time was speckled with interesting, strange, and unbelievable stories from real cases. Class ended five minutes early so that the teams could meet and exchange the needed information for setting up study groups.

Cindy, Tara, and John were on the case of the missing Mrs. M. They had managed to find out the make and model of the vehicle and believed that, with one more letter, they would have the personalized plate. Interestingly enough, they each had a different missing letter.

"I think before we meet, we should review each other's notes," Tara stated.

"Good idea," John agreed. "If I give you my notes, can you get copies?"

"Or we could use the post-and-patch technique and share our information as if we were all real investigators." Cindy wanted to jump right in. If they waited for copies and for people to read the copies, it would be several days before they would meet for the first time.

"But we've all gathered basically the same information," John rebutted.

"Again to my point. Why should we read the same thing we've written two more times. If we each share one piece at a time, we can add differences and not be repetitive on the things that are the same." Cindy was always looking for the fastest way to do everything.

John and Tara looked at each other as John's alarm rang, warning him to head to his next class.

"I'd like to meet to cover team ground rules," John insisted.

"I think we should work through all of the information one time," Tara replied. It was only going to be a quick review, but Tara was a thinker. She needed time to think about and adjust to the way the others processed the information. A quick review would provide Tara with an insight into the others.

They gave their contact information to Cindy. "I'll call you when I get a war room scheduled."

Cindy had become very excited in class when the instructor shared about the "war room" technique. It was a dedicated, secure space that looked like a war was in progress as the agents dug through data finding the pertinent truth.

"John, I know you're in class, but we have meeting room G3 for tomorrow at 3:00 p.m. for an hour. See you there!" Cindy had quickly found a room and set up the first meeting.

ꕤ 8 ꕤ

EVELYN WAS BUSY SORTING a batch of women's and children's clothes that came in that morning. One of the pieces caught her attention. *This looks like one of the pieces that came in with Mrs. M.'s last drop off. Just when I've stopped dwelling on Mrs. M.* It hadn't worked, however.

The more dead ends I run into, the more important it becomes for me to find out the truth. Unlike any of her other fun fantasies that she had created this story was drawing her to the truth. She had become obsessed with trying to find Mrs. M. It was almost as if the story itself was demanding the truth.

Evelyn picked up the last piece from the table. She marked it and hung it on a hanger, then took a step back from the racks. *Darn, I've been so wrapped up in my thoughts that I didn't properly sort the clothing.*

She took a few more minutes and reworked her sorting. Then Evelyn stepped out into the main room to find someone to help her move the two racks.

As Evelyn stepped out, she saw Travis walking towards the back of the store. She instantly felt her hopes raise and a smile formed from ear to ear. Maybe today was the day she would find out all of her answers. Travis waved, and Evelyn returned the wave as she quickened her pace.

"Travis! It's good to see you. Have you heard anything?"

"I was surprised you haven't called in a long time. Have you given up?"

"No. But I felt like I was being such a nuisance. I've imposed on you so much with this story."

"Imposed? No, don't feel that way. You've got me tied up in the curiosity of it. Mr. Thompkins, the instructor, called. He's caught up in it, too. He can't wait to find an answer. Several of his students are researching it, and he's been digging around, too. He dropped off this packet for me last night."

"What does it say?"

"I thought we could look at it together. Can you break for lunch?"

Evelyn looked at her watch. She had lost track of time. It was five minutes to her scheduled lunch break. She didn't need to think about it. Lunch today was being spent looking at the information in the packet. Evelyn nodded, then headed towards the back room.

"Hey, Matt," Evelyn called, "I've got a favor to ask."

Matt was working alone in his office as Evelyn walked by to check out for lunch. She normally had half an hour for lunch, and it always felt rushed if she left the building. Today she was going to be leaving, and she really wanted to go through the paperwork without pressure.

Matt looked up from his work and raised one eyebrow. "Life always gets interesting when you ask for a favor."

Evelyn knew from the look on Matt's face that he was curious and ready to consider her request. "Travis is here with information from the class trying to help track down Mrs. M. Can I have an extended lunch break?"

"What's the back room like?"

"I just finished hanging the last open rack. I was coming out to get help moving the full racks to the stocking area when I saw Travis."

"I only have one other issue."

"What's that?" Evelyn was worried by the look on Matt's face. She only saw him look like that when he turned people down.

"You didn't invite me."

"You've been complaining all week that you're too swamped with work to even take lunch. You're more than welcome to come with us."

"Where are you going?"

"The sub shop across the street."

"I'll be fifteen minutes behind you. That way we can come back at the same time, and it won't be apparent to the others."

"We'll save you a place at the table."

Evelyn picked up her time card and checked out for lunch. When they got back, she had to remember to have Matt sign by her lunch break to show that he had approved the extended time.

"Let's go, Travis. I'm dying to see what they've found out so far."

"Don't get your hopes up too high. The instructor is still suffering from curiosity. I take that to mean the students don't have it totally solved yet."

Travis held the door of the sub shop for Evelyn. They each placed their orders and paid for them as they picked them up. Then they found a table.

"I promised Matt we'd save room for him at the table. He wanted to know where the investigation's going. He thought he'd be along in about fifteen minutes."

"Then why don't we eat first, and he can follow along as we review the packet."

"I would say that was why he gave us a fifteen minute head start. Why aren't you at work?"

"I had some comp time coming. We've been working ten-hour days finishing a project this week. When we finished this morning, the boss told us that we could all take off the rest of the day to make up for the extra hours on the other days. It saves them paying us overtime."

"Wow, that was perfect timing."

"I would've woke you up this evening if we worked another long day." As Travis finished his sentence, Evelyn started laughing so hard she was afraid she was going to choke on her sandwich. He was so excited about the package that she was surprised he hadn't woken her up the night before with it.

Travis finished his meal first. He ate so quickly he got the hiccups. By the time he had the hiccups settled down, Evelyn was finishing her meal.

"Let me get rid of these trays. Why don't you open up the packet and see what we have," Evelyn said to

Travis. Matt walked into the restaurant as she stood up from the table. He waved to her, and she acknowledged the wave with a nod. Then she quickly took care of the trays and headed back to the table.

"Okay, let's see what we have here." Evelyn reached out towards the packet sitting beside Travis.

"You can wait just a few more seconds until Matt is sitting down." Travis gave Evelyn a mischievous look and pulled the packet away from her.

Matt glanced over towards the table as he was filling his soda at the self-serve fountain. Evelyn was wiggling like a four-year old waiting to open a Christmas present. She was sitting with both palms facing up and flittering her fingers at him signaling him to "come here quickly."

"Travis, you'd better open that up before she has a heart-attack," Matt said as he approached the table.

Travis opened the packet and pulled out three reports. Each report was titled, "The missing Mrs. M." and had the class name and student's name listed on the cover.

"How do we want to do this? Do we each take one and review it? Or do we look at them one at a time?"

"I vote we review them one at a time. It'll be faster, and Matt's still eating."

Evelyn tilted her head towards Matt who had just taken a big bite of his sandwich.

"Uh huh," Matt mumbled through his mouth full of food. He didn't dare try to say anything more.

Travis opened the first one. He was a bit of a speed reader and skimmed the first page. "The first page summarized the information given to the student and the approach chosen to search for Mrs. M. Local newspapers . . . hospitals . . . death notices at the court houses . . . Wow, this student came up with a few avenues you missed, Evelyn."

"What did they find?"

"I'm getting there. Oh, for the vehicle, they enlarged and modified the plate. Here are three possibilities that all seem reasonable from the blurry information, although none of them came up with anything positive. Then there's a blowup of Mr. M. The angle's bad and the photo blurry. The note indicates that the photo may be used as confirmation at a later date. But at this point, it was not helpful."

"Are you telling me that the first student didn't find anything?"

"Yup. Although the student hasn't given up and there are a couple of other items to be pursued."

"Like . . . ?" Evelyn tried to pull the rest of the sentence out of Travis.

"It looks like the student doesn't believe that the case is real. There's mention about looking in a different state, that maybe the items were dropped off at this Goodwill to throw the authorities off the case."

"On the front page did it note that Mrs. M. was a regular at the Goodwill?"

"Hmm, Let me see." Travis flipped back to the summary information. "No. It looks like this student didn't have that particular bit of information. Maybe I missed telling them." Travis made a note for Mr. Thompkins.

"Okay what does the second report show?" Matt asked between bites.

Travis quickly reviewed the information. "The second student came up with one more license plate option. There's a computer rotation of Mr. M. and trying to create more of his face. Oh, this is interesting."

"What?" Evelyn was ready to grab the report from Travis.

"There was a bit of a reflection of Mr. M. on the window of the car. Here's the recreation of the reflection." Travis held up the recreation for Evelyn and Matt to see.

Matt started choking on his sandwich. Evelyn just started laughing.

After he stopped coughing, Matt said, "That's me. I was standing just outside of the camera's range. There were a few shots with me in them, but Mr. M wasn't in them so I didn't give them to you."

Travis took the report back and flipped the page. "The student wasn't able to find a match of your photo in any of the databases. Good, you're not a criminal," Travis teased. "But it looks like he's certain that you are Mr. M."

"Won't he be surprised," Matt said matter-of-factly. "So, did the third student come up with anything new?"

Travis was skimming through the information. Most of the information was the same on the report. "This student not only got an analysis of your face, but there's also blow-up analysis of the side-view mirror and the parking tag. You can't tell where the parking tag is from, but it's green and hangs from the mirror of the car."

"I've seen tags like that on cars going through the drop off in the past. I'll have a couple of workers watch for them, and we'll see if there's just one place or several places that have similar tags in town. Can I get the blow up from you to leave as an example?" Matt asked as he finished his sub.

"Mr. Thompkins said that I needed to give this packet back. But I'll take this photo to the copy shop and have a color copy made for you."

"Anything else in the report?" Evelyn prompted, hoping to redirect him back to the report and to another tidbit of information.

"Nothing else. By the way, all three mentioned checking out-of-state plates next. Since they obviously checked out all possible matches in state, maybe that's a good choice." Travis tried to sound encouraging.

"Evelyn, did you ever think that maybe Mr. and Mrs. M. have a seasonal cabin at one of the nearby lakes?" The thought had just passed through Matt's mind. It was off-the-wall but not impossible. There were a lot of fancy lake homes in the area. Then he looked at his watch. "Time to get back to work."

"Travis, thanks for bringing the information over. At least we have a few more angles to consider. Parking lots for parking permits and people who live in the area in seasonal homes." Evelyn sounded encouraged despite the difficulty of being able to find either of the two newest clues. They left the sub shop and headed back towards the Goodwill.

"I think when I return the reports, I'll give a hint to the professor about our clues. Maybe they'll be able to tap into electrical bills or other information for homes around the lake that we wouldn't be able to check out as private citizens."

"Wonderful idea, although I'm sure that Evelyn's going to try her best. Evelyn. Back to work."

"Yes, sir."

9

JOAN HAD BEEN SWAMPED AT WORK. She hadn't taken time to go on her first break and was totally surprised when she heard everyone else starting to clear out for lunch. She was working on a project that needed about ten more minutes for completion. She decided to stay and finish it. By the time she would arrive at the cafeteria, the lines would be shorter.

The hairs on the back of her neck raised in the quiet of the office. It was an unsettling feeling. Joan regularly worked in the office when no one else was around. The silence in itself shouldn't bother her. Joan tried hard to put the unsettling feeling out of her mind. She focused on finishing her project so that she could head to lunch.

"Excuse me."

Joan jumped as a man's voice boomed loudly and confidently behind her. "I didn't mean to startle you. I've been watching you work for the past several minutes. You were so very focused I almost hated to interrupt you. Let me introduce myself—George Bartholomew III."

"Yes, Mr. Bartholomew. I recognize you from our company newsletter. How may I help you?" Joan never expected to find herself face-to-face with the director of the company. He was often in and out of town on business. This was the first time that she had seen him in person.

"I understand you're getting married soon," Mr. Bartholomew said in a casual tone.

"Yes, sir. That's correct." Joan was amazed he knew such a personal detail about her or that he stopped by to chat. He seemed too dignified for small talk.

"You didn't invite me." The tone in Mr. Bartholomew's voice was disappointment, almost hurt. Joan felt terrible. To be honest, the thought had never crossed her mind. But she didn't dare say that to him.

"My apologies for the oversight. If you will allow me, I can correct that right now." Joan wanted to tell him that the invitation list had been kept very small, that she and Jeremy were paying for the wedding themselves and didn't have the money for extra guests. Instead, Joan slid open the desk drawer to her right. She had brought an invitation in to work and had left it there.

She checked to make sure the RSVP was in place. Then she labeled the envelope "Mr. George Bartholomew III and guest." Luckily she had been told that his wife was deceased. It saved her from making a very embarrassing mistake by writing "Mr. & Mrs."

Joan stood up and faced Mr. Bartholomew. "It would be my pleasure to invite you to our wedding. I apologize for the short notice. But it would be an honor if you could attend." Out of a strength that Joan didn't know she possessed, her words came out clear, formal and confident. It was so opposite the knotted shakiness she was feeling inside.

Mr. Bartholomew accepted the invitation. He slid it open to check the date, smiled and nodded. "I will put it on my calendar. I'm not good at responding, so let this be my confirmation to attend. Now, may I ask you a couple of quick questions?"

"Certainly."

"Is it true that you're refusing to put any of your wedding on a payment plan? That if you can't pay cash up front you're going without?"

"Yes, that's true."

"Tell me how are things going?"

"Everything is paid for except—" Mr. Bartholomew broke in before Joan could finish her sentence.

"No. Tell me the details. Were there any special surprises?"

Joan recapped the highlights of the wedding planning in a quick five minutes. She still did not believe that Mr. Bartholomew wanted to chat about the personal details of her life. She shared the discount prices of the flowers, the women at work volunteering to do so much at the reception, the miracle of finding her gown for so very little that she had extra money for the honeymoon. Then receiving an extra thousand dollars for the honeymoon.

"So, it's true then. I overheard some women talking in the cafeteria one day. I wasn't planning on sitting down for lunch that day, but I found a table near enough to hear their conversation, and I eavesdropped. I know, shame on me. But my wife was quite the romantic. What I heard the women saying was just the romantic kind of story my wife would have loved."

"It is true," Joan told him and paused in thought, "Funny, I don't think of it as romantic. In fact, I was feeling like a bit of a miser."

Mr. Bartholomew smiled at Joan and allowed her to refocus before he said, "I need to go. But let me add another something special to your planning. The day that you have set aside for finalizing your honeymoon, contact my secretary. She has contacts at all the travel agencies. Tell her what you want, and she'll make the calls and get you a little better rate. I'll bring your agenda and tickets to the wedding for you."

"Thank you. We'll do that," Joan said softly as Mr. Bartholomew reached for her hand, shook it and left the office.

As Mr. Bartholomew walked away, Joan's coworkers returned. Joan, in shock, was still standing as everyone came in.

"Joan, is everything okay?"

"What did Mr. Bartholomew want?"

"Is someone in trouble? No, he looked happy. Did you get a promotion?" The questions seemed to be flying at Joan all at the same time from every direction.

"He invited himself to my wedding. Then he said we were to bring in our money for the honeymoon to his secretary on the day we had set aside to choose and that she would get us a better deal and arrange things for us." Joan hadn't picked up on what Mr. Bartholomew really insinuated. She had been so nervous that she had difficulties keeping her thoughts on her own words so that she didn't babble like a fool. His words had been totally misunderstood.

"Really?"

"Wow! That's awesome!'

"So, is he coming?" They all asked different questions at the same time again.

"I wish you'd all ask your questions one at a time. Yes and Yes," Joan responded to the questions and pointed to the person whose question matched her response. "I think I'm still in shock. Why does he want to come to my wedding? Before I wasn't embarrassed about how little we're doing. Now, I'm very embarrassed."

"Don't be. I walked in before the others did. I heard him tell you that your wedding would've been the romantic story that his wife would've loved. It sounds like he's only interested because of exactly what you have planned. So enjoy yourself and forget who he is or he's not going to be happy with you." Joan's boss always had a unique view of things, and he had been in meetings with Mr. Bartholomew, so Joan trusted his advice. "You missed your morning break and lunch. Take a break now so that you can concentrate the rest of the afternoon. We have a meeting in an hour and I need you focused."

Joan smiled at her boss as he turned around and walked back into his office. Joan picked up her purse and left for the cafeteria.

Forty-five minutes later, Joan came back from lunch break. She decided to cut her break fifteen minutes early because she still had a small portion of her project she wanted to finish before the afternoon meetings.

Joan was glad she had left a little work for just before the meeting. Her mind was racing in twenty directions after her meeting with Mr. Bartholomew. She needed that project to redirect her focus back to work. Although it did help, she still found herself more distracted than normal during the meetings.

Joan forgot about all of the stops she was planning to make on the way home. She raced home and ran for the phone.

"Answer, answer, answer," She chanted, each time she heard the phone ringing.

"Hello," Jeremy's roommate answered.

"This is Joan. Is Jeremy there?"

"He just drove up. Are you gonna hang on? Or should he call you back?"

"I'll wait for him. I'd pace even more if I were waiting for the phone to ring." Joan was pacing with the energy of excitement. She was charged. One part of her wanted to jump and dance with excitement. She had to tell Jeremy about the last wedding guest.

"Jeremy! Joan is on the phone. She sounds excited." His roommate yelled to him without moving his mouth away from the phone.

"Thanks, that just took care of my hearing for several months," Joan teased.

"Oh, sorry, Joan. I forgot. Here's Jeremy."

"Hi, Joan. I wasn't expecting you home for a couple of hours with all the stops you were planning. Is everything okay?" Jeremy was truly concerned.

"Yes, everything's wonderful. I feel like jumping with joy and yet at the same time I'm so nervous I can hardly stand it."

"Slow down. Start from the beginning. What's happened?"

"I was at my desk working on a project and getting ready for lunch. Everyone else had already left for lunch. Mr. Bartholomew, the director of the company, stopped by my desk to chat."

Jeremy could tell by the excited tone in Joan's voice that this wasn't an everyday occurrence. "To chat?" Jeremy repeated. "Isn't he too busy to chat?"

"I know!" Joan answered with an amazed acknowledgement. She was still in a bit of shock. "And do you know what he wanted to chat about?"

"Your outfit?" Jeremy said teasingly.

"Almost. Our wedding." Joan stayed silent for a few seconds letting that absorb. "He invited himself to our wedding and then wanted to chat about the details—flowers, dresses, reception—all the little details. Just like he was one of the girls at the lunch table."

"Are you pulling my leg?"

"No, honestly. We chatted for over half an hour. At the end, he said that when we chose our honeymoon location we were to let his secretary know and she'd take our payment and set it up for us. He said she's got connections and can get an even better deal for us."

"Wow! That's awesome."

"I'm so nervous now."

"Why?"

"He's going to be at our wedding."

"He chatted like one of your lunch buddies. He's just another guest."

"Keep reminding me of that, will you?" Joan said in an exasperated tone. Jeremy chuckled. "I suppose. I'd better take off again and run those errands. I'll call you later."

"I love you, Joan, and don't worry. I'm sure that Mr. Bartholomew wouldn't want you to worry about it. I'll be waiting for your call."

∞ ♦ ∞

Earlier that day, unbeknownst to Joan, Mr. Bartholomew called his secretary, Misty Dalton, whom he called Miss D, in for a private meeting.

"Miss D, I finally found Joan today. Next Thursday's the day they've set aside to choose their honeymoon. It sounded like they really didn't care where they went. I want you to begin planning an Hawaii vacation for them, and I'll be paying for it. When they come in, you can tell them you found an excellent deal and sway them to make Hawaii their decision."

"Did they say when they planned on leaving and when they planned on coming back?"

"You always think of the details. I thought to tell her that you have special connections. I also told her to contact you. I don't think she would be alarmed if you called and asked her the details."

"Does she know that you're paying?"

"I didn't mention it. But I also didn't mention anything about the two of them paying. I did tell her that I would bring the agenda and tickets to the wedding for them. We can cross that bridge when we come to it. Tours, I want at least two one-day tours pre-paid into the package, at least two of them, and at least one luau."

"I'll find out how many days they plan on being on their honeymoon. We don't want to over plan their time if they are only going to be there three or four days."

"What makes you think that they won't take a week to ten days."

"She's taking off two unpaid days before the wedding according to the rumor mill, and she only has 3.6 days of vacation to take."

"Transfer 6.4, no, 8.4 days of my vacation into her vacation account today. Print it up and find a way to pass it to her supervisor so that she can start thinking a little bit bigger."

"What if her fiancé is limited to the amount of time that he can take off?"

"You'll find a way around that, too. Use my name. Let me know when you've found something out. That's all for now."

Misty had a lot more issues that needed to be addressed. But she knew from what he had already said that she was to handle it. Whatever it took.

⁂ 10 ⁂

CINDY, TARA, AND JOHN, will you three please stay for a short meeting after class," Mr. Thompkins announced at the beginning of class.

The three students all acknowledged the request and looked at each other for some hint about the unusual meeting. "Do you think I pushed too hard for clearance of the computer system?" Tara asked Cindy. She also wondered if the others in her group were crossing that line also.

Class seemed longer than normal that day for Cindy, Tara, and John. There was mutual relief as they all gathered around the instructor's desk at the end of the class.

"The case you're working on is an unusual case. There are a group of three citizens also working on the case. There's not enough evidence for them to call the authorities, and they don't have the same resources you have, so you have come up with a few interesting findings they didn't. The case has not yet been solved. Since I can't get the two groups together, I reviewed your findings with them."

"What did they think of our preliminary findings?" John asked with interest.

"Ready to take notes? This is what you're to be told." The instructor paused as he waited for each of them to open their notebook. "It's a local case. Go ahead and do footwork: visit the Goodwill, check out local parking lots for the Mercedes. Go from there."

"Can we do interviews?" Tara asked.

"I don't see why not. Just remember to identify yourself as a student. We don't want anyone accidentally thinking that they're being investigated. Another fact that they felt needed to come out was that Mrs. M. was a regular to the Goodwill. As she changed her wardrobe for the season, all her old clothing was brought in. Flags were raised when, in the middle of the season, a gentleman brought in all the woman's clothes, costume jewelry, even her underwear."

Cindy and Tara both wrinkled their noses in disapproval. "Underwear? Ehw." They were about to change the discussion to how inappropriate that was when the instructor forced his way back in and continued his direction.

"Because Mrs. M. was a regular, they're saying that the out-of-state license plate idea must be wrong. I think you need to follow that through to its natural end. There will be some leads that look false and are true and others that look strong that will turn into wild goose chases. For this case, follow every lead to its natural end. Another lead that the civilians don't have the ability to check is going be difficult for you also. I want to meet with you in four days to see what you've found out."

"But what's going to be difficult for us to check into?" Tara asked with confusion.

"If I told you that, it would be too easy. I think that it's where you'll find your answer. But the direction itself can be found by following the clue that the case is local. If you aren't from the local area then you'll need to look into the local area," the instructor said as he talked to them in riddles. "Thanks for staying. I'll talk to you after class in four days."

As the instructor packed up his notes and books from the class, the students held an informal meeting.

"Interviewing class showed that it was best to interview with at least two people," Cindy said.

"I don't have a car. But I can ride with anyone else. My schedule is pretty open the next two days," Tara replied.

"I have two classes," John said, and he flipped out his schedule.

"I'm in one of those classes with you," Cindy said as she pointed to the one she was in.

"And I'm in the other one. What if we spend a couple of hours after each class interviewing? Maybe all three of us can go together?" Tara didn't want to be left out.

"I'll drive on the day I have class. Can you pick me up at my place on the other day?" Cindy asked to John.

"Sure. Give me your address, and we'll pick you up. Otherwise we'll meet at the front door of school right after class."

Everything was set up. The interviews would start the next day.

꧁ 11 ꧂

MATT, HAVE YOU EVER NOTICED how many different parking permits there are around town?" Evelyn asked.

"I've caught myself watching parking permits, too," Matt said thoughtfully. "They hang from the rear-view mirrors, in the corner of the front windshields, or the back windshields. They're all different sizes and colors."

"This has been a bit frustrating and at the same time exhilarating." Evelyn looked like a child waiting to open birthday presents. Matt smiled then nodded in agreement and headed back to his office.

Evelyn's focus wandered to her other stories. None of them had ever taken on a life like this one did. Nor this quickly coming to life. She was beginning to think she was going to crack if she didn't find out the truth soon.

At the same time, in the parking lot three students were getting out of the car. Tara, Cindy, and John walked into the Goodwill store together. There was one employee behind the till and another one working with the clothing on the racks. Tara was chosen to do the first interview.

"Excuse me," Tara said to the cashier.

"Yes? How can I help you?"

"We're students working on a class project. We were wondering if the person in this picture looked familiar to you?"

"Yeah, it looks like the store manager with a wig."

"Is the manager in today?"

"I'll check. Wait here, please."

The employee left the three students and went into the private office area. "There are three students out in the main area with a photo of you in a bad wig."

That statement alone was enough to make Matt smile. He did his best not to break up laughing. "What do they want?"

"They'd like to see you in person, I guess."

"Tell them I'll be right out." Matt finished up what he was doing and locked the confidential papers in his desk drawer before heading out. This was going to be interesting.

"Hello. My name's Matt. I was told that you were looking for me."

"My name's Tara. This is Cindy and John. We're students doing a research project. Would you have a few minutes for us to interview you?"

"I can give you about five minutes."

"This is for a class project. Is it okay if we tape the interview?" Tara had turned on the tape player in time to record her question.

"Go ahead, I don't mind if you tape it."

"You resemble the man in this photo. Is that you wearing a wig?"

"No. That is not me wearing a wig," Matt decided in a split second not to offer the students more information than what they asked for. He wanted to see how quickly they realized that the question was too narrow.

"Are you the man in this picture?" Cindy took the photo from Tara and presented it to the manager.

"It looks like me."

"This is the original picture." Cindy took out the picture that showed Mr. M from a hair-only shot. "Do you see the reflection in the glass?"

"Yes, I do."

"We have enlarged that reflection," Cindy said and switched back to the original photo. "This photo. Is the face in the reflection with the hair of the man that we can see? Are you the man whose face is reflecting in the window?"

"Yes."

"Can you show us where you were standing?" Cindy forgot to finish her sentence. She meant by pointing to the picture.

"Follow me." Matt walked out to the receiving area. The students looked confused at first. But they followed him. "I was standing about here."

"Where was the other man standing?" Cindy asked.

"He was about here."

"Did you know the other man?"

"No, I didn't."

"You're the manager. Is that correct?" John asked.

"Yes, I am."

"Do you frequently work in the receiving area?"

"No."

"Do you remember why you were in the receiving area that day?"

"I think I was covering for someone on break."

"Would it be possible for us to talk to the person who normally does the receiving."

"He's off-site on break right now. This is his break relief. She normally restocks the racks." Matt was hoping that one of the students would ask to talk to Evelyn. But he didn't want to openly direct them to her. It was the leadership quality in him that he wanted them to ask and learn.

"Is there anyone else you know of who might have seen anything that day?" Tara asked with uncertainty in her voice.

"I can give you a list of employees who worked the day these photos were taken," Matt said as he thought, *Good, Tara. You almost have the right question. Ask it again.*

"Our project is titled 'Find Mrs. M.' I guess what I'm asking is if there's someone here who knew something more about the man in the photo or his wife?" Tara was speaking slowly, thoughtfully.

"The employee you walked past on the way out here has often sorted through Mrs. M.'s drop-off items. She has never met Mrs. M., but she may be able to help you discover some things about her. Please wait here one moment." Matt stepped inside and spoke to Evelyn privately.

"Evelyn, these are the students whose reports we've read. You can't let them know that you've read the reports. And I know you want to feed them all kinds of information, but don't tell them anything they don't ask you about."

"But . . ."

"I'll be listening. You have ten minutes." Matt stuck his head out the door and motioned to the students. "Evelyn, this is Tara, Cindy, and John. They're students doing a research project. I know you're busy here today, but if you could take ten minutes to answer some questions for them."

"How can I be of help?" Evelyn asked.

"We've been assigned a research project called finding 'Mrs. M.' This is for a class project. Is it okay if we tape the interview?" The tape player was still running. Evelyn agreed, and John continued. "This is a picture of Mr. M and his car." John showed Evelyn one of the original photos. "Are you familiar with Mr. or Mrs. M. at all?"

"Sort of," Evelyn hesitantly answered.

"Have you ever personally met Mrs. M. or talked with her?" Tara asked.

"No, we've never met or talked."

"How do you know her?" Cindy inquired.

"Twice a year, at about each season change, one of the guys would come in with a big load of clothing and tell me, 'Mrs. M. just dropped off her clothing.' I always put everything else aside and sorted through her clothing."

"What made her clothing special?" Tara asked.

"Mrs. M. bought a new, full wardrobe twice a year. Sometimes there would be new tags on one or two pieces. She always brought in clothing that was not too aristocratic but very stylish and always in excellent condition."

"Do you remember when she was in last?" John asked.

"Normally I would be expecting her in any day. So I guess it was about five to six months ago."

"Normally," John said thoughtfully. "Why aren't you expecting her in any day now?"

"Mr. M. dropped off all of her clothes a few months back. In the middle of the season."

"Tell me about the last drop off," Tara said. "Was anything else unusual about it other than the fact it was in the middle of the season."

"Yes. He even dropped off personal items: bras, underwear, slips, and formal gowns. She rarely got rid of her formal gowns, and there were a large number of them in the clothing dropped off. The most surprising item was a man's tuxedo."

"Do you sell second-hand underwear?" Tara was appalled.

"Yes, as long as they are washed and in good condition. Truthfully, though, this was the first time in all my years that I've seen underwear dropped off."

"Are any of the items still in the store?" Cindy picked up, giving Tara a few minutes to regroup from her disgust about the underwear.

"That would be impossible to tell. We don't track clothing like a consignment store would."

Cindy looked at some of the pieces of clothing lying on the table. She picked them up and began to inspect them. "I would guess that you can tell a lot about a person by the things they drop off."

"It is sort of like talking to someone on the telephone and then finally meeting them. We make a lot of assumptions, but that's all they are."

"Can you share some of your assumptions about Mrs. M.?" Cindy knew that the assumptions would be far from fact. But maybe as the woman talked, something would come to light that would lead them in another direction.

"The first assumption was that she was rich enough to drive a Mercedes and change her complete wardrobe every season. Her clothing was never stained or the least bit worn. She kept a few transitional pieces each year, items that weren't as tied to a definite annual style. Other than that, there wasn't clothing from a different year. She always had the most up-to-date styles. She probably had a full staff of servants, a main residence, and at least one vacation home." Evelyn took a moment to reminisce.

"Sometimes she would drop off decorating items from home parties, just purchased and still in their boxes. So she must have had friends who she felt obligated to go to their home parties and purchase items. I would guess that her home was decorated by a designer and in a classic fashion with art work that didn't go in and out of fashion."

"Did she have any children?" John asked when Evelyn seemed to be running out of words.

"There weren't any children's clothing. If she had children, they were grown adults."

"What can you tell us about her size and weight? Do you remember what size clothing she wore?" John was trying to get Evelyn away from the subjective assumptions and try to build a physical image of Mrs. M.

"She was an average height and weight. I don't remember the exact size. But I never thought of her as excessively thin or overweight. There were three gowns I remember very well. They went with the tuxedo I mentioned. As I said, it was the only piece of men's clothing. The styles of the formal gowns made them timeless beauties. The first dress was pale-green with forest-green trimmings. The second dress was a soft shade of pink with a burgundy sash and burgundy decorative stitching. The third gown was a soft iridescent blue so pale that it looked like a blue light was reflecting off a white gown. The tuxedo had four accent colors: the traditional black, forest green, burgundy, and dark blue."

"These items got your attention more than the other pieces. You can still describe them. Did you keep track of them?" John had to try again to find a way to track the pieces.

"Yes, a bride and groom came in looking for a suit. I was able to show them the tuxedo, and they purchased it and all three dresses for their wedding. The bride remarked that two of the dresses would work as bridesmaid's dresses with minor alterations. The third dress fit her perfectly. I asked her to drop off a photo after the wedding."

"Has she done that yet?" There was hope in John's question.

"Not yet. I was just thinking about them this morning. I was trying to figure out if the wedding was last weekend or one of the two upcoming weekends. It's soon anyways."

"Anything else about the colors of her clothing?" Tara asked.

"No oranges, but otherwise she had a very colorful wardrobe. There were a great number of items still with full or partial tags on them. We assumed that it was so early in the season that she hadn't gotten around to wearing them yet."

"What would you guess her age to be?" Tara asked.

"I never physically saw her. But she was a woman at a status level that she didn't dress with her age in mind. She dressed for the event of the day. She had enough clothing to put on one outfit in the morning, change to go to lunch and change again for supper."

Just then Matt came around the corner. "Sorry to interrupt you, but we need to get Evelyn back to work."

"Thank you for your time," Cindy said for the entire group. Then she pulled out two school business cards with all of their names and numbers on the back. "If you think of anything else that you think might help us find Mrs. M., please feel free to give us a call." Cindy handed the cards to both Evelyn and her supervisor Matt.

Evelyn and Matt watched as the three students left.

"They are very green," Matt commented once they were out of hearing range.

"I tried to give them lots of hints, but they seemed to miss them all," Evelyn confirmed.

"Yeah, I know, I was listening." Matt smiled at her.

"I know."

12

SHOULD WE TAKE A FEW MINUTES to go over our notes and brainstorm?" Cindy asked after everyone was in the car.

"I think that's a good idea. I feel we got blown off course when the man in the window reflection turned out to be the store manager," Tara stated. "I have a poster-board at my place that I'm using like a white board with sticky notes. We can use that for our war room."

They all agreed and set off for Tara's place. No one talked during the short drive. They were all busy going over the interview and the notes, mentally preparing for the session ahead. Once at Tara's place, Tara handed out pads of sticky notes for everyone.

"Okay. What do we know that's new?" Tara started the discussion.

"High society. She might be in the society pages," Cindy offered.

"If she was that high society, then her death notice should have been in the local obituary," John was quick to point out. "None of the obits panned out. We've already checked that."

"I only went a month back before the start of class. How far back did you go?" Cindy asked.

"A month before class started," John said and Tara nodded to confirm that she had done the same.

"Okay, we can take our timeline back to the last season change that would have required a wardrobe change." Cindy stood up and extended the timeline back several months. "I'll check the social pages and obituaries. It'd help to see one of the formal dresses Evelyn described."

"I'll check the current engagement and wedding announcements and see if I can find out whose wedding it may be," Tara volunteered. "I'll go online while you two keep talking."

"Where did Mrs. M. live?" John was thinking out loud. "We've talked about the fact that she might not have been from this area or even this state. What if the clothes were from her vacation home in the area?"

"Oh, wow!" Cindy and John looked at Tara. "Look at all these weddings. There were six last weekend and more each of the next two weekends. I know there are about 50,000 people in this city, but I guess I'm just starting to realize the dynamics of our search."

"Let's quickly look through them." John redirected his thought pattern. "Did any of the weddings that have happened describe the bride's gown as any of the three purchased from the Goodwill?"

"Nope. All white or off white, nothing else."

"Can you print off the remaining notices so that we can group them and have the photos?" Cindy asked. Tara printed them, and they quickly cut them apart. Then they grouped them by ethnic origin.

"I don't remember Evelyn stating an ethnic origin on the couple. We have three different groups here. We can cut the list of people to check into just by knowing the ethnic background," John said as he put the clippings into groups on the table.

After reviewing the announcements, they decided that it was between three different couples, two Caucasian and one black. The church and location of the receptions meant that the weddings were probably not the frill and show that the other weddings would be. Although, it was a risk to make that assumption, it was a starting place for them.

"Tara, why don't you follow up with Evelyn on the couple then follow up with the couples," John continued. He really wanted to work the angle of the vacation house. "That pulls us back to where does Mrs. M. really live?"

"Talk about looking for a needle in a haystack. With all of the lakes in this area, how are we going to determine whose places are year-round homes versus vacation homes?" Cindy was overwhelmed by the thought.

"Some are registered as homesteaded verses non homesteaded, electrical bills, heating bills," John said, starting to roll off ideas.

Still overwhelmed, Cindy tried to add her viewpoint back into the picture. "From the amount of clothing Evelyn said was dropped off twice a year, I don't think the electrical and heating bills are going to be very effective. I would guess that they spent at least half of their time in the local area."

"We can't discount any possible idea. The obvious and the unlikely ideas should be checked out. So far we haven't done too well looking outside the box. I can't begin to count how many times I've heard the instructors say that we need to get outside of our boxes." John was getting frustrated. They all were getting annoyed with each other.

"I get the feeling that we've picked up the real mystery," Tara piped in.

"You have a real knack for seeing the obvious. I would guess that's why we got pulled aside and given a bit of direction," Cindy added sarcastically. "I'm shot for today. Let's get back together tomorrow."

They all nodded in agreement and began picking up their notes. They had found a few leads to follow. But for the most part, they were very frustrated. None of the leads were going to be easy to follow.

After everyone left, Tara called the Goodwill store. "Is Evelyn available?"

"No, she's already left for the day."

"Could I speak with the manager on duty?" Tara followed up. She was starting to get anxious.

"This is Matt. How can I help you?"

"This is Tara. I'm one of the students who stopped in earlier today. We have one more question."

"Okay, I'll try my best." Matt was hoping for more than just one more question.

"Do you know the ethnic background of the couple who purchased the tuxedo ensemble? We're trying to look in the society pages for one of Mrs. M.'s dresses," Tara explained.

"The couple was Caucasian," Matt answered.

"Thank you," Tara replied. "We appreciate your extra time." That narrowed the search from three to two or fifteen if the assumptions they made as they culled the others weren't correct.

꧁ 13 ꧂

As Joan got to work, her boss stopped by. "Can you come into my office for a moment?"

"I'll be right there." Joan got up from her desk and headed into the private office. She felt as if she were being called to the principal's office. "Do you want me to close the door?"

There were meetings with the boss, and then there were private meetings with the boss. Joan couldn't tell by the tone of voice how private this meeting was going to be.

"Please close the door, then have a seat." There was a pause in the conversation while Joan closed the door and took her seat. "Last night before I left, personnel stopped in with this paperwork."

"That can't be right. I don't have twelve days of vacation. I only have 3.6 days."

"I was distinctly told that you have twelve days and if you don't use the whole thing for your wedding and honeymoon you'll personally offend someone very high up in the company." He gave her a look that she'd better get the drift. "Start planning how the others can pick up your work for the extra days. You'll be gone just over two weeks."

"But . . ."

"Will Jeremy have problems getting that time off from work?"

"Probably. He hasn't even tried. He took a full week after the wedding so he could move. The bigger issue is that we can't afford a honeymoon longer than what we have planned. We can barely afford the airfare and hotel for the days we want as is."

"Call Jeremy from work. Have him try to get off another week. If he has problems, he has to call me and give me his boss's name and telephone number." Before she could even get a word out he finished. "No 'buts.' Just do as I say and don't question me. That's a direct order. It looks like you'll have time to help Jeremy move."

Back at her desk, Joan called Jeremy. She tried to explain what had happened. She didn't know herself what the whole thing was about. Jeremy wasn't working in a professional job yet. He worked a lot of hours in retail. The deadline had already passed to get additional time off, and he feared there was going to be trouble.

"Joan. They won't let me off. I'm only scheduled for three days and then only if I can find substitutes, I can get off. So far everyone I've asked has said no. I don't feel right about giving your boss my boss's name and telephone number. This doesn't sound right."

"I know, Jeremy. But I get the distinct feeling, it'll cause major problems with *my* job if we don't do this."

"Do you know what's gonna happen?"

"No. I'm afraid to ask. But, I've got to believe that they won't do anything to jeopardize your job." Joan and Jeremy finished the phone conversation. Jeremy reluctantly gave Joan the information that her boss had asked for. In turn, Joan gave the information to her boss and included on the slip the three days and times that Jeremy was scheduled.

Several hours passed uneventfully until Joan received a call from Mr. Bartholomew's secretary. This was going to be a day to test Joan's stress level.

"Hello, Joan. This is Misty Dalton, Mr. Bartholomew's administrative assistant."

"Yes, how can I help you?"

"I was wondering if I could get a list from you of the travel agencies you've contacted and the vacations that you're watching the prices on? That way I can put my contacts into place and on Thursday when you make your decision, it'll be easier to finalize plans."

"We were told that if a lot of people are looking for last minute deals, it'll backfire on us."

"Not a problem. I'll make sure they know that this is for the two of you. They'll also be more open to me about the chances of getting a good deal."

"I'll bring the information down at my next break, if that is okay?"

"That'll be fine. Also, can you tell me when you plan on leaving and when you plan on returning?"

"We were planning on leaving here on Monday morning and coming back on Wednesday evening. But somehow that's changed now. I guess we'll be staying longer, although I won't know for a couple of days how much longer."

"What do you mean?" Misty was trying to play dumb so she could find out how much Joan had been told about what was happening.

"My supervisor just told me that I had to find coverage to be out of work for *two weeks* around my wedding. I thought I had 3.6 days available for our honeymoon, but I just found out I have twelve days, though I don't know how. We only have the money we've saved to spend on the trip, so more days won't really matter. Depending on what deal we get, I may be helping Jeremy move in for a week. He had originally taken off a full week after the wedding and I had three days off. The other three days he was going to move. He's trying to get more time off so that his time matches my extended time, but it doesn't look too promising."

"I see. So when does he have to be back to work with the time he has off now?"

"If we fly out on Monday, then we could fly in on Sunday, and he would still make it to work on time. He only has three days of work that following week: Monday, Thursday, and Friday. So, if worse comes to worse, we can move some of his clothes before we leave and the rest of his things on Tuesday and Wednesday. Maybe it'll all work out."

"It always seems to, doesn't it? I'll see you later today with your lists."

"Thank you."

"You're welcome. Hopefully, it will alleviate some of your stress. You do sound very stressed right now."

"You're very perceptive. I am stressed. But I need to get back to work. I have a meeting in fifteen minutes."

Joan got a bit more work done before heading to the short meeting. As soon as she got out of the meeting, she ran copies of her honeymoon file to Misty Dalton's desk.

There were only a few days left before they needed to decide. Joan wasn't going to take the time to follow up until that Thursday. Misty told her not to worry about it, that she would have the options available for her.

"I can meet you off-site on Thursday to find out your choice if it's more convenient for you," Misty offered because it was a day off for Joan.

"We'll come by here," Joan said. She already felt guilty using Misty's time. They set up a time for her and Jeremy to come in and meet with Misty that was convenient to Misty's schedule.

Unbeknownst to Joan, Misty had the information from Jeremy's boss before Joan made it down with the rest of the information. Misty knew Jeremy's boss personally, and she didn't hesitate to pick up the phone and make a huge political move.

Jeremy was at work when Misty called. His boss called him into the office. "There was an error made in the schedule. You have a full week more off than what you were originally told," he said without tipping his hand.

"Uh . . . thank you," Jeremy said stunned by the information. Something was up. There was no doubt about it. But what was going on? With just a few days before the wedding and packing taking much longer than he expected, he wasn't about to complain. He could use all the extra time off that he could get. He was going to miss the added income, but with Joan not needing to take two unpaid days off before the wedding, it would all come out in the wash.

⁂ 14 ⁂

"This is my roommate, Jeff. He's going to help us today," John announced and gave Cindy and Tara a map of the town that had grids marked. "If you two can cover this section of town and the west mall, we will cover the east mall and this area here."

They were going to be looking for the parking permit the hard way. "Call us if you spot anything, and we'll do the same." If they found the permit in the shopping complex, they would need to trace the car to find out where the driver worked.

The boys were methodically going through the businesses in their section of town. The girls had a method of their own. But they had arranged it so that they would hit the shopping complex early in the search. It was an unofficial contest.

"John, it's Cindy. We found a parking permit, it's not the Mercedes but it's promising. We're calling in the trace next." The girls found the first parking permit in the window of a car.

"Good luck. We'll keep looking just in case your find doesn't work out."

They called it into one of the friends who had agreed to wait in the research lab and run plates for the two-hour hunt. “Ready for the trace? The license plate KJL 555.”

As they were waiting for information on the plate, a woman came out with a child and her arms full of packages to the car. The girls let her get her child and most of her packages situated before interrupting her.

“Excuse me, ma’am. We’re students doing a research project. We’ve been trying to trace this parking permit.” Tara showed the woman the photo of the permit in the Mercedes. “It appears you may have a permit from the same lot. We were wondering if you could tell us where it’s from?”

“My husband just bought this car over the weekend. I really don’t know where it is from.”

“Do you know who he bought it from?” Tara continued while Cindy answered the phone and then whispered a name to Tara.

“I don’t have any idea, and I don’t have the title. My husband was going to be transferring the title today.”

“May I ask what your last name is?”

“Johnson.” Just then the child started screaming and yelling. “I really need to get going. It is past her nap time.”

“Thanks for your help.” Tara turned towards Cindy. “Well, no simple answer, but the name on the plate wasn’t hers. So, if we can track down the former owner, we may have a chance.”

“Let’s hold off on that for another day. We can keep looking for active leads.”

The girls got back in their car and drove around the rest of the parking lot. They took a moment to call the guys and tell them that they had their first hit. But it would take further research and it held no easy answers.

"I tried to place calls to the two couples last night. I reached one person. A couple getting married this next weekend." Tara took advantage of the time they were driving around to update Cindy.

"I hit the jackpot on finding the three gowns." Tara slid the wedding announcement for Joan and Jeremy out of her portfolio. "This is the couple who purchased them. Today is the bride's last day at work this week. She's working late and will be off at five. If we're there when she leaves, she'll talk with us for a couple of minutes. Do you have the time this evening?"

"Where is it at?"

"Manufacturing Plus corporate office across town on River Street."

"It would give us an idea of the size of Mrs. M. so that we have a little better idea of who we're looking for."

"The bride, Joan, said she would be willing to give me a photo they took the day of the fittings. It'll have all three dresses. We'll have a good photo to look at before starting through the society pages."

"That makes me feel a little better. It's the first sign that maybe things won't be totally out of reach. John was going to start working this evening on his search of vacation homes in the area."

"How is he going to do that?"

"With the help of Craig, who was born and raised in the area, they've picked twelve neighborhoods where they're going to begin doing searches. John has the research computer signed out for two hours tonight and three hours each of the next two days. I guess they're going to start gathering information about the homes and families in those areas."

"Did John want help?"

"No, I offered. But he said the search he was doing was too complicated to explain. Besides, he was only able to get one computer."

Two hours of driving, and there weren't any more hits. Both cars came up dry. They agreed that Tara was going to call the former owner of the first car later that evening if the phone number was listed.

"We have an hour before we can go by the Manufacturing Plus corporate offices. How 'bout catching a bite to eat?" Cindy asked Tara.

"I have a whole three dollars on me. I guess that means fast food."

"Works for me."

As much as they tried to stretch it out, they were in and out of the fast food restaurant in half an hour. They had each had a cheeseburger and fries from the dollar menu. It was enough to take the hungry edge away.

They drove around and checked out a few more parking lots on their way to the appointment. They didn't want to be too early. At the same time, they hoped they would accidentally get lucky.

As they drove into the parking lot at Manufacturing Plus, they had to check in at the guard's desk. True to her word, Joan had notified the guard that Tara was expected. They were given a pink tag to place in the windshield of the car with a big number on it. As they left, they needed to turn the tag back in to the guard's desk. But until then, it was the one thing that would keep their car from being towed.

"Over there," Tara said as she pointed. "That's the building she told me to meet her in front of."

Cindy drove over to the visitor parking area in front of the building Tara had pointed at. There were a lot of open parking places because it was so late in the day. Cindy and Tara were so distracted, they didn't notice the other cars in the parking lot, all of them with the same exact parking lot tag that they had been looking for all over town.

"Do you think I should let her know that I'm here?" Tara asked.

"Was she going to meet you or were you going to call to confirm. We're still fifteen minutes early, you know."

"We were going to meet. I just can't sit still any more."

"Let's get out and walk closer to the door." Cindy got out of the car. But instead of walking towards the door, she walked to the next row of cars. "Tara! Look at their parking tags."

"Oh, my word!" Tara exclaimed with excitement. "It can't be, can it?"

"Let's check with the receptionist before they lock the doors for the day." As Cindy said that, she dialed John's cell phone number and left him a brief message. "Hey, John, we are at Manufacturing Plus corporate offices for our meeting about the formal gowns. I think we hit the jackpot. The parking permits seem to match the one in our photo. We'll let you know what we find out. Bye."

Tara was already through the doors and at the reception desk introducing herself. "Hello, I'm Tara. I'm a student doing a research project. One of our clues is the photo of this car. The parking permit in the window matches your corporate parking permit. I was wondering if you recognize this car?"

"No, I'm sorry, I don't. But I've only been working here for about a month. Maybe the guard station can help you?" Tara's excitement deflated immediately. The guard had told them that they would need to leave their parking permit in the drop box because the guard station was closing in five minutes. That meant that it was already closed. Cindy heard the receptionist's response and put her hand on Tara's shoulder.

"I guess we can come back here one of the next two days," Cindy said to Tara. "We're here to see Joan. Can you tell her that we are here?"

"Do you know Joan's last name? Or what department that she works in?"

"No, she left our name at the guard's station. When we told him, he didn't ask for a last name."

"His information is organized by time of day. You were probably the last one's on his list to check in for the day. I'm sorry. But we don't have any visitors showing here that we're still expecting. We lock the door in about two minutes. We'll have to have you wait outside unless you know Joan's last name or the department she works for."

"We can wait outside. She had told us to wait for her by the front door. I don't think it matters if we are inside or outside."

"I'm sorry I couldn't be of more help."

"Don't worry about it." Tara and Cindy picked up their paperwork and headed for the door with the people who were walking out to their cars. A steady stream of people had been exiting since they arrived. They had to step back several feet when the mass exodus began minutes later.

As Tara watched people exiting through the glass doorways, she noticed a young woman inside the lobby looking around. The young woman was holding a photograph. "Cindy, let's go back in quickly."

With that Cindy and Tara pushed their way against the stream of people to re-enter the lobby area. Traffic slowed as confused people began splitting to either side of them. It caused such a commotion in the lobby that it caught the young woman's attention. Joan stepped through the traffic and shepherded the two women out of the traffic and off to the side.

"Is one of you Tara?" Joan asked.

"Yes, I'm Tara and this is Cindy. Thanks for meeting with us."

"I don't have long. I have about an hour of work left and then I leave on vacation. I'm getting married on Saturday."

"Congratulations! As I explained on the phone, we are doing a school project called 'Finding Mrs. M.' It's led us to the tuxedo and three dresses that you purchased from the Goodwill. They belonged to Mrs. M."

"Here is a photo of the three of us in her dresses after they were altered. They were all custom-made dresses."

"If I may ask, what size do you normally wear? It will give us an estimation of the size of Mrs. M."

"I'm five-seven, and I usually wear a size twelve. How is her size and the photo going to help you?"

"From the things we know about her, we're hoping to be able to find her in the society pages of the paper. Either she or her husband may have worked here. We just realized on the way in that the parking permit in their car was from here."

"What's the number? I may be able to help track that for you," Joan offered. She knew she would need to get permission before she gave out this kind of information. Then she realized it would be absolutely amazing to find out that her wedding party was wearing the dresses of one of her co-workers.

That didn't make sense, though. The photo had been taken and shown to so many people in the office. If the dresses belonged to someone at work, they would probably have said something about it.

"Here's a photo of the car. This is the blow up of the permit. We've enhanced it to show the numbers."

"Oh." Joan sounded disappointed. "There's only the first three numbers in the permit. We use all the same permits at all of our locations. This narrows it down to about a thousand people." Joan gave the girls half a smile. Her disappointment showed on her face.

"Have you ever seen the car before?" Cindy asked hoping that they may have a lead.

"I'm sorry. I don't pay too much attention to cars, and I haven't worked here very long. Maybe the guards tomorrow will be able to help you."

"Are there any people from work going to your wedding this weekend?"

"A few. But they've all seen the photo, and no one has said anything. So I don't think that there'll be any new leads for you from my wedding. I'd like to hear the results of your project, though."

"Here's a school card. It has all three of our names on the back." Joan squinted her eyes at Cindy like she was crazy. There were just the two of them standing there. "We have a third person working with us. He's doing research on vacation homes in the area. Anyway, it has the school number and our home numbers in case you think of anything else."

"Here's my card." Joan had thought to bring one of her business cards with her from her desk. She picked up a pen from the front desk and wrote her home phone number on it. "Please leave me a message when you find Mrs. M. I'm curious now to know whose dress I'm wearing for my wedding dress."

Joan had to use her security pass to open the doors for the girls to leave. They had chatted for so long that the guard had locked them in the building. After the girls were gone, Joan went back to her desk to finish her work.

❧ ♦ ☙

"Tara, do you have plans for the evening?"

"No. What were you thinking?"

"John's due at the lab in fifteen minutes. Let's fill him in on what we've found."

"You know the way he is. We'll have to keep it short so we don't impose on his research time."

Tara and Cindy got into Cindy's car and drove over to the school. The excitement was building. They had real hope that they were going to be able to find Mrs. M. before the project was due in two weeks. One of the other teams had already reported a solved case. That meant the pressure was on for the other teams.

It was after normal school hours. There were a few night classes going on as the girls ran down the hallways to the lab where John was working. They burst through the door with such excitement that everyone stopped what they were doing and looked up.

"We found the parking permits!" Tara and Cindy said at nearly the same time.

"Where at?" John turned his focus away from his PC search and notes.

"Manufacturing Plus. But there wasn't enough of the permit showing to see who the car was registered to. The guards were already gone for the day. If we go back tomorrow, they may recognize the vehicle. But they have several locations, and the same permits are used at all of them." Tara said this so quickly that John almost didn't catch everything.

"Do they have locations out of state?" John asked. Cindy and Tara looked at each other, then back at John. Each girl shrugged. They hadn't thought to ask. Actually, they didn't have time to ask because they had arrived at Manufacturing Plus at closing time.

John turned back to his PC and entered new search parameters. Cindy and Tara moved in to look over his shoulder. "Sixteen locations in ten states. The headquarters is . . ." John skimmed the screen in front of him. "Yup. Here in town. Okay. I'm going to see what I can find out about the top officials of the company. They're people who fit the profile. They might work at multiple locations or work at another location and come to town frequently enough for meetings that they'd have a second home in town. That changes my search. It should narrow down the list. Thanks, now I feel like I may find something if I can cross reference the people on this list with local property owners."

"We're almost there. Let's go back to my place and work on the PC there for a look at the social pages," Tara said to Cindy as they left.

15

JEREMY WAS BUSY PACKING. He had lost track of time and jumped when the phone rang.

"Hey, Jeremy." Joan was home from her long, last day of work.

"Sweetheart. What time is it?"

"Almost seven. I know. I worked later than I was supposed to."

"I'd lost track of time. I can't believe how much I have to pack up."

"Are you still going to make our meeting with Misty tomorrow?"

"Yes. I'll be there. I'll pack my car full if you have time to help me unload it at your place."

"What were you planning on bringing over?"

"My suitcase for the honeymoon. Some books."

"I guess we can move a carload full. How are you packing for the honeymoon if we haven't chosen where we are going yet?"

"I've packed a pair of underwear, my swim suit, a set of clothing for warm weather and a set of clothing for cold weather. What more do I need?"

Joan rolled her eyes. "Please tell me you are joking."

"Okay, maybe it was four pairs of underwear and a couple of outfits for warm weather," Jeremy said with a smile. He knew he was pushing her buttons. "I'm not packing much but most of the places on our list would be warm during the day and possibly cooler at night."

"I've been over our list time and time again. I don't know how I can choose if more than one destination comes in under what we can afford."

"As long as I'm with you, I don't care where we go," Jeremy said and as the words came out of his mouth a wild idea began to form in his mind. "Joan, let's not decide."

"What?"

"How about this? Everything that qualifies we put in a separate envelope. We draw out one envelope and hand it to Misty to make the arrangements. Every one's so curious about where we're going. We'd be able to honestly say, 'I don't know.' How cool is that?" Jeremy paused for a minute giving Joan time to think about the idea.

"Well, Joan? Do you think that you can stand the suspense?" At first all Jeremy heard was a sigh on the other end of the phone.

"I've made so many decisions preparing for this wedding, I don't want to make another one. All of the places on our list are nice places to go. My absolute dream would be to go to Hawaii. But we have less than half of what we need for that trip. I like your idea. It'll be a surprise for both of us."

"That sounds good to me. What are you planning to do for the rest of the evening?"

"Eat a quick supper and then I guess I can start packing for the honeymoon. I haven't watched TV for quite a while. I thought that I might spend a couple hours just vegging out."

"You veg-out? I'll believe that when I see it. I know you. You'll have your checklists in front of you and be double-checking them instead of watching the show."

"Oh, you're probably right. But in the end, I'll be more relaxed and have a game plan for the next two days. I love you so much. I almost wish we could skip the whole stressful wedding."

"Take tonight and get rid of the stress. I'd bet if you look at the source you'll realize that you're most stressed about getting ready for the long vacation from work."

"Yeah, you're right about that."

"Goodnight, Sweetie."

"Goodnight." It was difficult for Joan to hang up the phone. She longed to at least be talking with Jeremy. She couldn't wait until she would have the comfort of his love at the end of every day.

As Jeremy predicted, Joan spent the evening watching TV and going over her checklists. She put together the list of places she needed to go to the next day. She had them broke down to A, B, and C priorities, just in case something took longer than predicted. There was still much to be done in a very short amount of time.

Jeremy and I made a pact to do whatever we could afford to do. I'm adjusting it tonight to whatever gets done, gets done. If I don't have time to get it done, it just wouldn't be a part of the festivities, Joan told herself as she went to bed that evening.

The next morning, Joan met Jeremy at the front desk of Manufacturing Plus. They walked together to Misty Dalton's desk. Jeremy wanted to reach out and hold Joan's hand the way he normally would. But everything was so stanch and professional that he was afraid of embarrassing Joan in her workplace.

"Hello, Joan, and you must be Jeremy. Nice to meet you." Misty picked up a stack of papers from the corner of her desk. She immediately ushered Joan and Jeremy into the small conference room beside Mr. Bartholomew's office. "I've been able to get several excellent deals for you to choose from."

"We decided that we can't make any more choices." Joan pulled out six small envelopes from her purse. "If you could put each good deal under our price limit in a separate envelope, then we'll choose an envelope and it will be a surprise for us when Mr. Bartholomew passes us the information on Saturday."

Misty smiled. This was going to work out better than she had expected. She already had the itinerary and tickets in her desk for the Hawaiian honeymoon that Mr. Bartholomew had requested. Misty picked up several of the envelopes and stuffed them. Then she held them up fanned out like cards in front of Joan and Jeremy. "Pick one."

Joan reached forward and picked out an envelope. She laid the envelope on the table. Then she reached into her purse and pulled out her billfold. From it she removed the amount that she had told Misty was their spending limit. There was an extra four hundred dollars that she would buy travelers checks with later that day.

"We forgot to ask if I should bring this money in cash, check, or a travelers check to you. So, obviously, I brought cash."

"That'll work just fine. I'll put any extra into travelers checks for you. I have some forms for you to sign that'll allow me to pick up the travelers checks." It should have raised questions for Joan and Jeremy that Misty had travelers check forms for them to sign. But they had so much to do that they didn't give it a second thought.

"Do you know that you'll for sure be stopping by the bank to get some travelers checks?" Joan asked sheepishly. Misty played the part and looked into the envelope they had picked. Then she counted the money on the table.

"Yes. There'll be extra money." Misty was about ready to die of anxiety. She wanted to share the secret more than anything at this point. Somehow from deep within, she found her composure.

"May I give you the extra four hundred and have you convert that as long as you're at the bank?" Joan felt like she was imposing on Misty. Without that extra stop at the bank, there was no doubt she would be able to get everything done on her list today.

"I can do that for you. That's not a problem for me at all," Misty said. She had wondered if Joan and Jeremy had considered spending money. Four hundred wasn't much for the places they had on the list. But none of that really mattered. They were going to have a large amount of spending money for Hawaii.

Joan and Jeremy signed the documents exactly as Misty had requested. It had all gone smoothly and quickly. Misty was actually going to be back from the bank before she had the meeting ending her schedule for the day.

"Since I have peeked, I can tell you that you'll have a fabulous time on your honeymoon. I'll have everything together in an envelope and send it with Mr. Bartholomew. Now, go and finish what you need to do today and have a wonderful wedding on Saturday." With that Misty reached forward and wrapped Joan in a big hug. Then she stepped back and shook Jeremy's hand as she sent them on their way.

Mr. Bartholomew walked out of his office just in time to see Joan and Jeremy walking away. "Did you have any problems?"

"Not at all. They decided not to decide. They put all of the destinations in envelopes and picked out an envelope. Then they set the envelope in front of me and announced that they didn't want to know where they were going. They want it to be a surprise." Misty smiled from ear to ear.

"They'll be surprised, won't they?"

"Yes, sir. I'll be out of the office for about half an hour. I'm going to the bank for the travelers checks."

"Do you have my travel arrangements in order for next week?"

"Where are you going?" Misty teased. "Just kidding. Yes, I do."

Misty picked up her purse. She put the money in an envelope with the travelers check documents and left for the bank. She had to pull some very difficult strings with her sister at the bank to pull off this surprise. She couldn't stop smiling. It felt so good to be a part of such a wonderful blessing.

ഌ 16 ൽ

FRIDAY JOHN, CINDY, AND TARa met at Tara's place to review their notes so far. After the excitement on Wednesday, they hadn't spent more time on the project. Between class schedules and work schedules, none of them had the spare time to work on the project.

"Okay. We know Mrs. M. had some kind of connection to Manufacturing Plus." Cindy wrote 'Mfg. +' on the white board. "What did you find in your search, John?"

"They have over two thousand employees locally. I was only able to get the names of the top three levels of management and board of directors. It's all information that's been in the newspaper over the last year."

"So some of the names may not be valid any more?" Tara prompted.

"That's a possibility, but not a high probability. I'm guessing that although others in the company travel, this group of people are the only ones in the company that might be able to afford a Mercedes."

"Okay. What have you been able to find out about them individually? Are there any who we can immediately eliminate?"

"This is a grid I did for some of the information we may be looking for: Property, specifically two homes in different states, and spousal or significant other information." John placed the large chart in the center of the table. Their heads almost hit as they leaned over the table and reviewed the chart.

"Mr. Jacobson, bachelor never married. We can eliminate him," Cindy stated.

"What if he was keeping a girlfriend at each of his three homes? The assumption was that Mr. and Mrs. M. were married. What if—"

"John, you're terrible! With a thought process like that we wouldn't be able to eliminate anyone of these people."

"That's what I'm saying. With the information we have here on this grid, we can't eliminate anyone. For one thing, I don't know that the marriage status is current. I think that's where we need to begin. We need to find a way to validate the marriage-status column."

"They all have either primary or secondary houses in the area. Some of them have three houses total." Tara looked amazed at the schedule. "Sorry, I just don't believe that some people live this way. I suppose we should also check to make sure that they're still with the company and still own the same homes?"

"Which column will lead us to the solution faster?" John didn't like Tara's trying to distract the team. Although that information may need to be validated, if the couple was still happily married, they could be eliminated. But if Mrs. M. was really a mistress, none of their presumptions would help. At this point, he just wanted to sift through the first level and leave the mistress possibility as a background note for the future.

"You obviously have an opinion," Tara snipped. "And I'd say that was your way of telling me to focus again."

"He didn't say that, Tara." Cindy tried to calm her down. "We don't have much time left. By checking to see if this marriage status column has changed for anyone, it will allow us to immediately cut out a lot of people. Everyone still married can be eliminated."

"Not if Mrs. M. was a local mistress. They may still be married, and it had something to do with an inappropriate relationship."

"We're talking in circles. Let's narrow the list down by validating any relationship changes over the past year. If someone doesn't stand out by that, then we can double check the property issue." Cindy tried to compromise. There were times when Tara couldn't grasp what appeared to be the obvious.

"We have enough base information to do a property search. But not enough to do a search on private information." Tara was trying hard to find another way to do the search her way.

John's cell phone rang. He was glad he forgot to turn it off. The interruption came at just the right time. As he glanced at the number, he realized it was his instructor.

"Hopefully this is our answer as we speak." John flipped open his cell phone. "Hello. Thanks for returning my phone call."

"Your message said that you need increased security access. Do you know where Cindy and Tara are?"

"They're here with me. We're all over at Tara's reviewing the information. We've come up against a dead end. We don't have a high enough clearance to validate the current marriage status of about two dozen people."

"I don't have another class for two hours. Can you pick up everything you have and do an impromptu presentation for me? If from your presentation I can see that you've narrowed the group to the most likely candidates and you don't have sufficient security, I'll use mine to print you the information you need."

"We'll be there in fifteen minutes." John hung up his cell phone. "We need to bring everything with us and do an impromptu presentation. The goal will be to demonstrate that there's a high confidence that Mr. M. is in this group and that we do not have the access to narrow down the field any more."

"Let's go," Cindy said. Tara began picking up some of the paperwork. She was silently pouting. But she knew she had just been out-voted.

They arrived at school and presented the information. It included the matching partial parking permit, income levels adequate to drive a Mercedes and multiple homes in multiple states. They explained that the greatest risk factor was if Mrs. M. was actually a mistress or a live-in girlfriend.

The teacher agreed that they were at a stopping point without the extended security. He took the time to sign on through the levels of the live database with his security pass codes. Then he picked up a stack of papers from the corner of his desk and moved to the worktable off to the side.

John, Cindy, and Tara all moved to the backside of the desk. John directed Cindy to work directly on the PC. Tara was slightly irritated, but she knew the instructor gave them a grade on professionalism, so she chose to keep quiet.

An hour later, they felt confident that they had the list down to three. The most obvious choice was Mr. Bartholomew. His wife had passed away unexpectedly in the last year.

After reviewing their schedules, they decided to wait until Monday to go to Manufacturing Plus. They were hoping to get to speak with Mr. Bartholomew directly. Their instructor warned them that they needed to make sure that they were very cautious. The man may not wish to talk with a group of college students about the death of his wife.

ꟷ 17 ꟷ

IT WAS THE DAY BEFORE HIS WEDDING. Jeremy had procrastinated as usual. He was just heading over to pick up his tuxedo from the dry cleaners. He had also had the other colors of accessories dry cleaned at the same time.

"I'm here to pick up my tuxedo," Jeremy said as he handed over the claim ticket he had been given when he dropped the clothing off.

"Here you go," the clerk said as they hung the bag off to the side of the register.

"What's in the manila envelope?" Jeremy was confused. There was a brown privacy envelope carefully taped to the bag that held the rest of the clothing.

"The cummerbund's are specially tailored. I've never seen anything like them before. They have secret pockets. There was a note tucked in each one of them. We put the notes in envelopes and sealed them in the manila envelope. I'd like to assure you that no one on the staff read any of the notes."

"I don't think that they're mine. I didn't know that the secret pockets existed. My fiancée sent the tuxedo with me the day we bought it. I doubt she'd have put notes in the cummerbunds."

"They came in your clothes. That means they belong to you. It's your choice if you want to throw them away."

As Jeremy drove away, he considered the clerk's words. He didn't think he would be able to throw away the letters. They needed to be read. But he wasn't sure he could invade someone else's private moments. He decided to tuck the letters into his shaving kit, the only piece of luggage not already at Joan's. He would show the letters to her as they flew to their surprise destination.

"Hey, hey, roommate, are you ready for this wedding tomorrow?" The best man said as he walked into the practice with his tuxedo.

"I'll tell you in a couple of weeks. Are you sure you'll remember to take my clothes back with you tomorrow?"

"Don't worry," he said off-hand, distracted by Amy and Sandy getting out of a vehicle with their bridesmaid's dresses.

The practice went smoothly. Joan was amazed how her nerves settled as she went through the steps. Everything on her checklist had been completed. She was excited about the wedding the next day. But because she was confident in her love towards Jeremy, she wasn't nervous about getting married.

They both loved God immensely and centered their relationship in him. It left no room for either of them to doubt their choice. The thing that was almost unbearable was that she did not know where they were going for the honeymoon. Strangely, she wasn't worried. Instead she was very excited.

Sleep was difficult that evening for Joan. She was so excited about the wedding the next day. She had been running literally non-stop for the past two days arranging all of the final details. She knew at this point if anything went wrong that there wasn't anything to do but roll with it. She wasn't worried; she was just so wound up from the past two days that relaxing into sleep just wasn't happening.

The red numbers on her digital clock changed from 11:59 to 12:00. She rolled over and stared at the phone. Maybe, just maybe, Jeremy was having problems sleeping, too.

Jeremy leaned over from his desk to grab the phone on his bedside stand as it rang just after midnight. "Hello?" He answered with confusion. Who would call at this time of night?

"Are you having difficulties sleeping, too?" It was Joan's soft voice on the other end of the phone.

"Yes. I was just looking at four envelopes."

"Four envelopes?"

"Yes, when I picked up my tuxedo, they told me that there were letters in each of the four cummerbunds. Did you put letters in them?"

"No, they're not from me. Did you say *in* them? Are there pockets?"

"I guess there's a hidden pocket in each one according to the dry cleaners."

"Did you read any of the letters?"

"No. I didn't think you'd had time to tuck notes into hidden pockets. So, I was thinking that if they were letters meant for someone else, I shouldn't read them.

But for some reason, I just can't sleep. I keep looking at the envelopes with the letters. I almost feel like they are calling me to read them."

"Oh, that is so exciting and romantic. Open up one letter and read it to me."

"Aren't we imposing on someone's private thoughts then?"

"Maybe if you read the letters, we'll know who they belong to."

"There is black, blue, green, and burgundy written on the outside of the envelopes. Which one?"

"Black. It would be the color that he may wear without her and one of her matching gowns."

Joan could hear Jeremy opening the envelope and unfolding the letter.

"To my beloved,

"I am not sure why. But I woke up tonight with a desperation in my spirit. I felt that I needed to write you a love note. I miss you when you're on these business trips. My heart yearns for its soul mate.

"I trust God daily to keep you safe when we're apart. I whisper words to the angels and ask them to whisper my love to you that you may always know that I am not complete without you. You are the treasure of my soul. We could lose all our money and possessions, and in your arms I would still find a full measure of love and joy.

"My spirit tonight is grieving. I don't understand why. I spoke to you just hours ago as you were getting up and I was going to bed. I have asked God,

'What is this grief I feel?' Separation is the word that comes flowing to my heart.

"On my knees I have pleaded with God not to take you from me. To bring you home quickly so this time of separation will be ended and I may feel your loving arms around me once again. I lay prostate, begging and crying for the protection of my soul mate. Yet the breaking in my heart does not receive peace. Knowing that God has heard my prayers for you. I write to you, my beloved, and thank you for filling my heart and life with such joy.

"For all these years you have made me complete. I love you with a love that shall have no end. Even when I sit beside Jesus in heaven, my heart will be tied to yours. You are my soul mate. My love for you abounds more and more each day. In telling you this, I now receive peace.

"With all my love, Elizabeth"

"Oh, Jeremy. We need to find Elizabeth's husband."

"Joan. This note is dated about a month before we bought the outfits at the Goodwill store."

"She must have died unexpectedly. Read another one."

"This is the blue one. It's shorter."

"That's the one that matches my wedding gown," Joan said reflectively.

"My beloved,

"Thank you for having made this gown of love. We lost our unborn child the month you commissioned this dress. And to my blue mood you added shimmer, light, and your never-ending love.

"You understood how difficult for me, under the circumstances, the month of planned social events was going to be. So you gave me my gown of hope. Now every time I wear this dress, I'll remember the hope of light that we find in Christ even when we are blue.

"Our angel is watching over us from the arms of Jesus. She will bless us with her unending love, a testament of our love together. She rains down upon us the hope that God has a blessing still in store for us.

"With all my love, Elizabeth"

"Joan? Are you okay." She had remained silent on the phone after Jeremy finished reading the letter.

"I don't know that I can wear the dress for my wedding gown."

"She called it her dress of hope. I think it's very appropriate."

"Read another one." Joan's heart was aching, yet the love portrayed in the first two letters mirrored her love for Jeremy.

"This is the burgundy letter."

"My Dearest Valentine,

"This is our fourteenth Valentine's Day together. I know without a doubt that you are the one and only Valentine for me. You are my soul mate.

"I'm not sure how it can be that I love you more with each passing year. Many people say that as a relationship grows older love changes. They mean that love becomes more soft, gentle and almost taken for granted. But for us, my love, it has become more passionate; it is a flower just beginning to bloom.

"With all my love, Elizabeth"

"The final one is the green one. Can you handle hearing one more?" Jeremy heard Joan crying and blowing her nose over the phone line. He was having a difficult time stopping himself from crying. It was obvious that these outfits belong to two people who had found more than love, they had found their soul mate.

"No. But read it. I don't think that I can rest without hearing it."

"My Dearest Love,

"Merry Christmas! May God's everlasting life fill you with joy and peace! I love you with all of my heart, with all of my life and with all of my soul!

"I am glad that we chose the day of eternal love to be married. I know that I have been one of the lucky few to find my soul mate. If the day ever comes that this life separates us, there will be no regrets, for God has blessed us by allowing us to share his eternal love with each other.

"With all my love, Elizabeth"

"Those letters are beautiful. Did I tell you that there was a group of college students trying to find the man who dropped off the outfits?"

"No, you didn't."

"I wish I had time tomorrow to call them. Maybe they've found him by now. Maybe there'll be an easy way for us to deliver these letters to him."

"As soon as we get back from our honeymoon," Jeremy assured her. "Good night now. We have to get some rest or we'll sleep through the wedding."

Both Joan and Jeremy fell asleep shortly after they hung up the phone. They had an early afternoon wedding planned. At least they could sleep in a little bit.

18

THE CHURCH WAS FULL AS Mr. Bartholomew entered a few minutes before the start of the wedding. He had hoped to sit inconspicuously towards the back of the church. The ushers kept politely asking people to sit closer together. The back half of the church was already overstuffed.

"The bride's side or the groom's?" The usher inquired as he approached.

"The bride's side. But, I can sit wherever it works best or on a chair in the back if you're going to extend some."

"Are you Mr. Bartholomew?"

"Yes, I am."

"The bride has reserved a seat for you in the second row."

Mr. Bartholomew wanted to tell the young man that it was not necessary. But he remembered his etiquette. He knew that this was Joan's way of making up for her perceived mistake of not inviting him.

After he was seated, the grandparents were escorted in, then Joan's mother and Jeremy's parents. It was a small wedding. The groom, his best man, and an individual groomsman came in from the side door, and the music changed.

It was obviously the processional music. The music and intimacy of the chapel reminded him so much of his own wedding. Despite his wealth, he had been married in a small, private, and old-fashioned ceremony. *It must be the reminiscent memory that makes this young woman look like my dear wife in her beautiful pale green dress with forest green trimmings*, he thought to himself.

The second girl passed by and a tear rolled down his cheek as he imagined seeing his wife in her beautiful pink gown with burgundy sash and the most beautiful burgundy decorative stitching. He tried to focus on the wedding instead of his personal pain. But instead he found himself thinking, "You were the most beautiful Valentine's Day Gala chairwomen ever." And he remembered how his wife tucked her head into his neck as they danced.

The organ blew a commanding sound that pulled him out of his little world. The bride was ready to come. Everyone stood and turned around to view the beautiful bride as her father graciously escorted her down the aisle to the altar.

Her dress was a beautiful white with an iridescent shimmer of blue. Joan had a smile from ear to ear. She was unable to contain her excitement. She nodded to her guests as she passed by. Then tears began to fill her eyes despite her ear-to ear smile.

Joan caught sight of Mr. Bartholomew. He was crying, tears running down both his cheeks. She didn't know why, but she shared his tears through her happiness. Joan's father slipped a handkerchief to her as he passed her to Jeremy.

When everyone turned back to face the front of the church, Mr. Bartholomew wiped his eyes. He wanted so much to slip out of the church. But he was so far forward it would be rude. As everyone sat down and the service began, he saw the whole picture for the first time.

"My dearest Elizabeth forgive me. In my mourning I cleared out your closets at the vacation house. I didn't realize the tuxedo and formal gowns were there." He thought prayerfully. "The prompting of my heart when I overhead the women talking in the cafeteria must have been your angel, whispering softly in my ear, urging me to find a way to be present here today. I know you're watching from Heaven.

He sat tearfully and quietly watching the rest of the wedding ceremony. *Elizabeth always called the blue dress her dress of hope, the red dress the symbol of her soul mate and the green dress the symbol of their eternal love. Yes, it is a fitting start for this couple to be surrounded by hope and love as they join together as soul mates.* He thought and smiled despite his pain.

Joan and Jeremy had decided to stand at the back of the church greeting their guests with their parents by their side. Mr. Bartholomew was one of the first ones to go through the line because of his seat of privilege. He gave Joan a big hug as if he'd been her father and not the virtual stranger to her that he was. It was obvious that he had cried through the entire ceremony. He pulled the envelope from his suit coat pocket.

"Enclosed with my card are your tickets, agenda, and travelers checks. Enjoy your honeymoon," he said softly and gently as he handed the envelope to Joan. She gave him another hug and a kiss on the cheek before responding.

"Thank you so much. It took so much stress out of my week not having to worry about the honeymoon plans. This is my husband, Jeremy. Jeremy, this is Mr. George Bartholomew III. He's the director of our company." After Jeremy shook Mr. Bartholomew's hand, Joan passed him the card to slip into his jacket pocket for safekeeping.

"It's my pleasure to meet you. I look forward to talking with you more at the reception."

"I wish I could stay. But business has come up that won't allow me to stay." Then directing his words to Joan he added, "You have the most beautiful wedding gown I've ever seen. And your bridesmaids are most lovely also."

"Thank you. The gowns have a story to tell and when we get back from our honeymoon, we need to look up the man who dropped them off at the Goodwill."

"Stop by my office, and I'll help you find him." Tears were beginning to well up in Mr. Bartholomew's eyes and with that, he turned and left the wedding, stopping only a short second to talk specifically to the fathers.

The reception was a wonderful time. Jeremy and Joan took a lot of time to visit with their friends. The bridesmaids opened up the wedding gifts, carefully recording each gift on the card. Towards the end of the day, the groomsmen carried the gifts up to the waiting truck. To their surprise, Joan's decorated car had been moved. Some of the decorations had been moved from her car to a Mercedes Benz.

After the last load was taken out to the pickup, the groomsmen came down to get the bride and groom. The guests had started to leave about a half-hour before yet they mysteriously all made their way back inside. Joan and Jeremy wanted to go but were feeling obligated to stay since none of the guests were leaving.

"Time to go," Joan's father announced. "Come on everybody. Let's go upstairs and send the bride and groom off in style."

Joan couldn't believe how every one seemed to rush out of the church. She and Jeremy found themselves virtually alone in the church basement. They looked at each other with a bit of confusion. But they had been looking for a way to leave for quite some time, so they followed up the stairs to the main entrance. As they walked out the back of the church, they froze in the doorway. There in the street was a Mercedes Benz. The best man, acting like a chauffeur, opened the back door and helped the bride and groom inside. Then he walked around to the front and drove away with them.

A processional of ten or more cars trailed through town beeping and waving. Joan felt like a queen. When they arrived at Joan's place, the parents had already unloaded all of the gifts into the apartment.

"Mr. Bartholomew said that you were to lock the keys in the car at the airport. It'll be picked up on Monday. He also said that Miss. D. would arrange for a ride home when you return," Jeremy's father said as the keys were passed to Jeremy. "So, where are you going on your honeymoon?"

"You know we've been so busy, I didn't even open the card to look." Jeremy slid the card out of his jacket pocket and passed the tickets and agenda to Joan as he took a minute to read the card. "Joan and Jeremy, Congratulations. I hope you won't be offended. I over-rode your choice and had Miss D. plan this trip for you instead, on me. All your money has been placed into trav-elers checks. Make the most of your trip, and don't save the travelers checks for anything. Aloha, George."

Jeremy looked over at Joan as she began unfold-ing the papers that he had given to her. "Hawaii! He's sending us to Hawaii for twelve days. It looks like we'll be doing some island hopping. Oh, my goodness!"

The conversation exploded into ten minutes of mass confusion as everyone shared in the excitement and managed to say good-bye, leaving Joan and Jeremy alone in the apartment. It had been a wonderful, happy day. Nothing had gone wrong except that it was only eight o'clock and both Joan and Jeremy found themselves exhausted.

"Now that we're alone," Joan said to Jeremy as they wrapped their arms around each other. "Let's take a nap."

Jeremy started laughing uncontrollably. "I was thinking the same thing." He picked her up and laid her down still in her gown on top of the bed, fully made. Then he lay down beside her, and they took a nap.

They woke up about an hour later, feeling refreshed and the honeymoon began.

၈ 19 ଓ

MONDAY MORNING AT Nine, the three college students arrived once again at Manufacturing Plus. All three of the men on their list who they wanted to talk with were out of the office.

The receptionist offered to call Misty Dalton. She guaranteed the three students that Misty would be able to convey a message to any of the three men. Misty was willing to break away from her day for a few minutes to talk with the students.

"Thank you for seeing us," Cindy started the conversation. She took a couple of minutes with introductions and explaining the project that they had been given. Then she immediately started showing the photos of the Mercedes dropping off clothing and the photo of the four dresses.

Misty immediately recognized Mr. Bartholomew and his vehicle. She also recognized his wife's dresses and her heart went out. She began to see the big picture. Joan wore Elizabeth's Hope dress as her wedding gown. No wonder Mr. Bartholomew hadn't stayed for the reception but had called her instead.

Misty filled in the rest of the story from Elizabeth's death to the wedding on Saturday. The students had everything they needed for their report. But there was still a piece of the story missing, the piece that had gone with Joan and Jeremy on their honeymoon.

Mr. Bartholomew woke up that morning in his main home. *Forgive me, Elizabeth,* he thought. *I know you liked the vacation home better. Maybe that is why I've been spending more time at our formal home.*" He took off for home after the wedding, making Misty re-arrange his travel plans at the last moment. He needed to work through some more of his grief.

When you died, I had a difficult time moving on. It wasn't that they had spent fifty or sixty years together. Their time together had been relatively short. But their love had been deep. *I suffered a heart attack just after you passed away. Misty had told me straight out that I had a broken heart and that Elizabeth would want me to heal it and not die.* Tears rolled down his cheeks for the third day in a row. He was finally letting go of his pain and tears.

"I was given the will to live. The will to fight to go on with life." He recalled that the week before his heart attack, he had dropped off his wife's clothes at the Goodwill. He had been trying to block all memory of her from his mind. He stopped grieving that day. Now he realized that he had to work through his grief. The part he played in Jeremy and Joan's wedding had opened the door to his feelings again.

"Jeremy, from the time we stepped off the plane in Hawaii we've been treated like royalty," Joan said with a smile. Misty had arranged for perks during their honeymoon that only top-level executives received. "I'm glad I brought thirty rolls of film and the digital camera we received as a wedding present."

"Mr. Bartholomew told you not to hold any travelers check back for any reason. Did you listen?" Jeremy asked.

"No, I left three hundred dollars at the apartment for developing the film. We filled up the camera and back up storage and almost ran out of film. I'm glad now I did that." It was the last day. They had done so much and seen so many new places and things. It was the trip of a lifetime.

Before leaving, they went to the post office and shipped back four good-sized boxes filled with souvenirs for themselves and family members. Per Misty's instructions, it was mailed to Joan at work.

"I can't believe it's already time to get onto the plane and go home," Jeremy said as they waited for the plane. Their honeymoon was just about over. They had almost been married for two weeks already. They read over the letters that had been in the cummerbunds almost every day. It was the love relationship that they strove to build. A triune relationship that, as they got closer to each other, they both got closer to God.

Exhausted, they both slept most of the way home.

Joan and Jeremy's plane finally landed. They claimed their luggage. "Look, that driver has our name on his sign," Jeremy said as they walked outside. A limousine driver was standing next to his car with their names on the sign. The driver checked Jeremy's driver's license to confirm that he had the right passengers. Then he loaded their bags and took them home.

"Tomorrow morning can we go to Manufacturing Plus to visit Mr. Bartholomew?" Joan asked.

"I think that's a great idea. We need to say a personal thank you," Jeremy said as he held his new wife close in the back of the limousine.

The next morning they found out that Mr. Bartholomew was in but very booked. Still, he chose to take a few minutes to visit with the newlyweds.

"Thank you for the wonderful honeymoon," Jeremy started out the conversation.

"It was definitely a trip to remember," Joan agreed.

"I need to explain to you why I left before the reception," Mr. Bartholomew said, very serious. There were almost tears in his eyes. "The dresses you and your bridesmaids wore were my late wife's dresses." With that he pointed to several photos on the bookcase. The photos were of Elizabeth at various formal events with him.

Joan took the letters out of her purse and handed them to Jeremy, who was sitting closer to the desk. Jeremy placed the letters on the desk. "Please forgive us for reading your private letters. That must be Elizabeth." Jeremy nodded to a picture that had been recently put on the bookshelf. George nodded in response. "She was beautiful. And she loved you very much."

"And I loved her very much. When she died, I almost died of a broken heart. I'm glad that you read my letters. It means that you found them and were able to get them back to me. Where did she hide them?"

"There are secret pockets in each of the cummerbunds. She had a different letter tucked in each one. The outside of the envelope shows which one and when she wrote it."

George looked at the envelopes. Then he noticed the black one had been written the day before she left on her last trip. He carefully took the letter out and read it while Joan and Jeremy sat in the office with him. As tears flowed down his cheeks, he finally said, "She wrote this her last day at home before she died. God gave her a warning without actually telling her. It was a car bomb that took her life, but it was her time. This final letter is as much a message from God as a message from her." George wiped the tears from his eyes as he softly spoke.

They talked for just a few more minutes then George gave both Joan and Jeremy big hugs before he sent them on their way.

The next stop was to drop the film off to be processed. The photos from the digital camera would be processed to fill in any missing or bad shots from the other camera.

Then they went to get the rental truck to move Jeremy. His friends were meeting them at his place that evening. The rest of his things were going to be loaded up that night.

"You macho men look like you have this moving thing under control," Joan said with a pleading look as Jeremy and his friends started loading the truck. "Is it okay if we go pick up the photos?"

"Like I could stop you," Jeremy said with a smile. He was as anxious as she was to see the photos.

Joan and her friends slipped away to pick up the photos. The Goodwill store was only two blocks away from the photo lab. So she dropped off a photo of the wedding party as promised. Matt, the manager was still on duty. He shared with the women the information from the report. Joan pulled the copy she had made of the love letters out of her purse.

"May I make a copy to keep for Evelyn?" Matt asked after he read them.

"They aren't really mine. We did give the originals to the owner," Joan said. Then with a cautious tone in her voice she replied, "I guess it would be okay. He wasn't upset that we had read them." Then she left her name and telephone number for Evelyn.

Matt didn't wait for Evelyn's next day of work. He called her at home. Per Matt's request, Evelyn waited until the next day to call. She and Joan talked for hours as they put the story together.

Epilogue

GEORGE BARTHOLOMEW III had married the love of his life, Elizabeth. They knew from the beginning that they were soul mates. Despite their combined wealth, they were married in a small church with only close friends and family present on Christmas Day, the day of eternal love.

Her wedding dress was a traditional white gown. But to commemorate their wedding, George had a pale green dress made by a top designer. It was a dress of classic beauty that would never go out of style. The intricate forest-green needlework trimmed the gown and added a touch of class. To Elizabeth, the dress meant eternal life and love.

Life was not always easy for them. They had difficulty conceiving a child. And when they did conceive, Elizabeth was unable to carry the child full term. She lost their only child, and the doctors told her that she would never be able to have a child. She referred to her baby as an angel of love.

Again, George had a special dress commissioned for her. The designer looked the world over for the perfect fabric. It was white like pure, fallen snow with a blue hue that shimmered when the light hit it just perfectly. To Elizabeth this gown symbolized how when pure love was added to a blue mood hope was produced.

The love between George and Elizabeth did not wax and wane but instead grew stronger and deeper with each passing year. They did not lose the romance in their relationship the way many couples did. Instead they recognized that they were soul mates. And through each season the love and romance in their marriage grew.

As a special Valentine's Day present, George had a third dress commissioned by a top designer. It was the perfect dress for Elizabeth. It was like a flower just beginning to bloom. Its soft pink material formed perfectly to her body. A burgundy sash adding depth and dimension and the beautiful decorative burgundy stitching was hundreds of open roses. To Elizabeth this dress symbolized their growing passion and blossoming love.

George and Elizabeth had two homes. Their primary home was a formal mansion with servants of every kind for every occasion. The vacation home was a smaller, five-bedroom home, with a guesthouse off to the side that was used for a married couple who was responsible for being a chauffeur when needed, doing grounds work, cooking and cleaning. Elizabeth preferred to live in the vacation home.

George traveled a lot with his job. Sometimes Elizabeth would travel with him. They longed to be with each other. They were both in agony when it didn't work for them to travel together. As soul mates, when they were far apart from each other, they would feel the pain.

They would often know when the other was sick or in need of help.

George was overseas on a business trip. Elizabeth couldn't leave until she had finished with the fundraiser that they had been working on for a year. After the fundraiser was over and she was going to be leaving the next morning, she found herself unable to sleep. She felt the soft prompting to write George a love letter.

That year for the first time, when they had put away the formal dresses and cummerbunds, she tucked a note in the secret compartment of the cummerbunds, a compartment specially designed per her request. The notes were not just simple notes, but love letters to touch the heart of her soul mate. She wrote the love letter that she was feeling prompted to write and placed it in the secret compartment of the black cummerbund. It seemed to fit because her soul was mourning. There was a grief she had never experienced before. Writing this final love letter brought peace to her grieving spirit.

The next morning, her flight took off as scheduled. Her plane landed on time, and she arrived at the hotel where her husband was staying. She went up to her room and took a short nap while waiting for her husband to finish his meetings. As she came into the lobby area to check for messages after her nap, a car bomb exploded. She lived just long enough for her spirit to be filled with understanding. Her grief was lifted and replaced with peace. It was George's grief that would live on.

George had a heart attack. He was literally dying of a broken heart. His soul mate, his true love was gone forever. Shortly before his heart attack, he had his servants load up all of Elizabeth's clothing and personal effects into the Mercedes. He dropped them off at the Goodwill. He knew that Elizabeth often took loads of clothing to the Goodwill. Then George went home for several months and left the vacation home in the competent hands of his servants, the couple that lived in the guesthouse.

Evelyn, longtime employee of the Goodwill store, needed to know what happened to the woman who had frequented the store with donations for years. The clothing somehow called her to find an answer. What had happened to the owner of the clothing? She hunted everywhere she could for answers. She even found a connection to an instructor at the local FBI academy. Three students chose to help find the answer.

They found out more than they bargained for. Life was creating a unique circle, tying itself together. Joan, a bride to be who worked for Manufacturing Plus purchased the dresses and the tuxedo. As Joan planned her small, romantic wedding, George Bartholomew III, the director of Manufacturing Plus, was drawn in by the romantic story. It was just the kind of story that Elizabeth, his deceased wife, would have loved.

He desired to make it even more romantic for the couple and give them a dream honeymoon. Little did he know, the wedding that he invited himself to was going to bring Elizabeth back to him. The memories and love of a soul mate would touch his heart. They flooded back as he saw the young women walk down the isle in Elizabeth's specially commissioned designer gowns.

Elizabeth's words blessed the couple on the eve of their wedding. And her words haunted the couple with a desire to find the soul mate of Elizabeth to deliver the love notes to their rightful owner, her beloved.

Upon their return from their honeymoon, Jeremy and Joan intended to begin the search for Elizabeth's soul mate. They stopped by Mr. Bartholomew's office to thank him for the wonderful honeymoon and to see if he was able to help them find out where the dresses had come from as he had offered to do at the wedding.

The circle came to a close as Mr. Bartholomew revealed that the dresses belonged to his wife, Elizabeth. Jeremy and Joan returned the letters to Mr. Bartholomew. After reading the letter Elizabeth had written the night before she died, George shared the tragic death of his wife Elizabeth with Jeremy and Joan.

In life we dance the dance of love, in a circle round we go. Our right hand on the shoulder of our neighbor as our left hand reaches into the circle, reaching for God. We know the ones on our right and on our left and yet we touch the lives of everyone when we reach into the center. It is the center of the circle that gives us the strength and holds us up when we get weary. We are never alone. We are all intertwined.

Evelyn